BEING MRS. CANE

SHANORA WILLIAMS

Copyright © 2018 Shanora Williams

All rights reserved. This eBook is licensed for your personal enjoyment only. This eBook is copyright material and must not be copied, reproduced, transferred, distributed, leased, licensed or publicly performed or used in any form without prior written permission of the publisher, as allowed under the terms and conditions under which it was purchased or as strictly permitted by applicable copyright law. Any unauthorized distribution, circulation or use of this text may be a direct infringement of the author's rights, and those responsible may be liable in law accordingly.

Thank you for respecting the work of this author.

Cover Design by Hang Le

Editing By Librum Artis

Trademarks: This book identifies product names and services known to be trademarks, registered trademarks, or service marks of their respective holders. The author acknowledges the trademarked status in this work of fiction. The publication and use of these trademarks is not authorized, associated with, or sponsored by the trademark owners.

NOTIFICATIONS

To get notified about new release alerts, free books, and exclusive updates, join my newsletter by visiting www.shanorawilliams.com/mailing-list

AUTHOR NOTE

Hey there!

Just a heads up, this is the last book of the Cane Series and cannot be read as a standalone. To read the first three books of the series, you can find them at

www.shanorawilliams.com/all-books

CHAPTER 1

ANDY

It's been eight weeks since Cane and I got back from Belize.

Eight weeks since I screamed the word *"Yes!"* while Cane was perched on one knee in front of me.

As a little girl, I used to dream about how he would ask me. Of course, back then I was delusional, and he had no idea that I loved him so deeply, but still—I always wondered how *the* Quinton Cane would ask a woman to marry him.

Would he make himself vulnerable by dropping to one knee? Would he look her in the eyes? Would he say something deep and sweet, or quick and simple?

I got the answers to all of those questions that night in Belize, and it was one of the best moments we've ever shared.

Marriage was a big step, one I hadn't mentally prepared for after everything we'd been through. To be honest, I was perfectly content with where we were before he asked for my hand in marriage. We were happy, living our lives, and enjoying one another's company, and that was all I'd ever wanted.

Take this very morning, for example. I was happy. Cane and I were in the bed, and I'd just begun to stir as the sun spilled over the horizon. He was sleeping, but when I ran a hand over his bare chest he groaned, and his eyes slowly peeled open.

"Mmm," he murmured. "Morning, little one."

There was always something about his voice in the morning. The extra bass to it—a gravelly-ness that made me clench. Yes, *clench*.

"You leave tonight," I said with a sigh. I wasn't too pleased about it. Then again, I never was. Every time he had to travel for work, I missed the hell out of him. He always extended the offer of joining him, but I didn't want to distract him. I knew work was work, and he needed to concentrate and be present for the majority of it.

"I'll be back soon," he rumbled. I climbed on top of him, swinging my hair to one side.

"You'll miss me?"

"Every second," he said, smiling as he clutched my hips. "I'll be thinking about you every day that I'm away. Thinking of all the things I can do to you."

"Oh yeah? Things like what?" I asked, biting back a grin. "Show me."

He didn't hesitate. He flipped me onto my back, and I let out a shrill yelp as he pushed up on one elbow, his face hovering over mine. His hand slid over my belly, moving down to my pelvis. He pushed his hand between my legs, and when I was exposed, one of his fingers skimmed over my bare pussy.

"Things like touching you here," he said, his lips above mine. "What else?"

He adjusted his body higher, sliding two fingers inside me. "Fucking you with my fingers," he rasped on my lips. "Feeling your wet pussy come all over them."

I moaned, and clenched again.

"What...else?" My voice was breathy—erratic—as he massaged my clit with the bottom of his palm, his fingers still penetrating deep. He continued the massaging a few seconds longer but then came to a rapid stop. "No," I whined. "Why did you stop?"

He didn't answer. Instead, he moved down between my thighs. "Would you rather have my fingers," he crooned, the head of his cock pushing into my pussy, "or my dick inside you?"

"Your dick," I panted as he stalled. I writhed a bit, aching for the rest of him, but he didn't budge, only chuckled.

"So impatient, little one."

"You know I am. Now stop teasing."

His eyes skimmed over me. "How do you want it?"

"Hard," I said, bringing my mouth up to his. "Fast," I added. "And deep." When that last word left my lips, I clutched his hips and forced them forward.

His cock thrust into me with ease, and a primal growl started deep in his chest, falling through his lips.

He dropped his head, crushing my mouth with his as I held on tighter. Rocking his hips back and forth, he gave it to me just how I wanted it.

Harder.

Faster.

Deeper.

He sucked on my bottom lip while I panted and moaned beneath him. My fingernails dug into the skin of his hips, and he released my lip with a hiss. His eyes latched on mine, and he brought a hand up, tangling his fingers in my hair. He grabbed a handful of it and yanked back just enough so my neck craned, and then sucked on the bend of it.

"Fucking mine," he growled on my mouth. "All of you belongs to me. Right, baby?"

"Yes. I'm all yours."

"*My* fiancée," he groaned, and his body tensed, muscles locking.

"Yours," I breathed erratically, and he grunted almost instantly. His cock pulsed inside me as he came, his eyelids sealing as one of his hands locked on my hips.

"Fuck, you feel so good," he moaned, pulsing, twitching. "I'll never get tired of this pussy."

When his body relaxed, he pulled out and then looked down at me, dropping a damp kiss on my lips. He gave me another, and I let out a whimper.

He dropped his hand and used the tips of his fingers to rub circles on my clit. My body bucked in response, and he swallowed my moans, still kissing me. Owning me.

His soft cock was now on my thigh, rubbing against me. I felt him spasm as he massaged me faster, building me up more and more.

"Oh, God! Cane!" I cried out. His hand felt so damn good, and my body had been worked up since the moment he'd thrust inside me. I clutched the sheets with one hand while my other ran through the hair on the back of his head, and then I came all over his fingers, just as he'd been anticipating, and he hummed in response.

"I'll never get tired of that either," he mumbled on my mouth, and I could tell he was smiling. "Watching you come for me."

I smiled up at him, and after we'd cleaned up what we could, we jumped in the shower together, this time making love. We always made love before he left town.

For some, marriage means harmony, but for Cane and I...well, I had no idea what it meant for us. To be honest, a part of me was afraid that one day he would want a family, and I wouldn't be able to deliver that.

Even so, not much had changed since we'd gotten engaged. We were still the same couple who loved too hard, and fucked even harder, even after getting back from our trip. I will say that my love for him was monumental—like somehow being engaged to him was deeper than just him asking me a question. It was as if we were connected by an invisible but unbreakable chain.

Once Lora found out, she asked if she could help plan our wedding, and when Cane and I agreed she could, she immediately started investigating options. She assured me the wedding wouldn't happen until after I graduated, and promised that the process would be as stress-free as possible, just so long as Cane didn't try and set a low budget for it.

Later that night, I watched Cane walk out the door to get to the black car that was waiting for him. Neo, his driver, stood patiently by the trunk with his hands clasped in front of him. Cane had given Neo his suitcase, but before he got into the backseat, Cane came back toward the porch, jogged up the steps, and reeled me in by the waist, giving me a passionate, sensual kiss. I giggled behind it at first, and then kissed him just as deeply, curling my fingers into his shirt.

"I love you, *girl*," he said, pulling away, walking backward before reaching the steps.

"And I love you, *man*. Safe travels." I blew him a kiss as he climbed into the car. Neo shut the door behind him, and before I knew it, the car was rolling away.

Sighing, I went back into the house and upstairs, where I spotted Lora coming out of her room.

"Hey munchkin!" she sang.

I laughed. "Hey. You wanna watch a movie tonight?"

"Kandy Jennings!" she gasped. "Are you asking me on a date?"

I broke out in a laugh, walking into my and Cane's bedroom. Lora followed after me as I walked to the closet and pulled out a blanket and my favorite pair of fuzzy socks.

"Just a movie, no play." I winked back at her.

"Sure, I don't see why not. Oh—I didn't even tell you about this bridal boutique I found. It's in Charlotte. I went to check it out, and the dresses are fucking *stunning*, Kandy. You'd love them."

"But are they super expensive?" I asked, pressing my lips and closing the closet door.

She scoffed. "Um, duh! I'm not letting you walk around in some two-dollar shit, okay? Only the best for you. Got it?"

I smiled.

"Now Cane…he's going to be a little harder to get in order. He'd settle for a basic-as-hell tux." Her head shook. "Not letting that happen. I mean, he's got all that money and is so cheap with it." She rolled her eyes as she fluffed her hair in front of our floor-to-ceiling mirror.

"You know we don't need a great, big wedding, Lora," I laughed. "I don't even know that many people—not any that are close enough for me to invite, anyway."

"Yeah, but Cane does, and once word gets out about him getting married, the people who work for him are going to be fighting to get an invitation. Did you see that Tempt has announced on their website and blog that he proposed to "a special lady" in Belize? I'm not sure how the word got out, but I'm sure his emails and calls are blowing up right about it now."

"Yeah, but just because he works with them doesn't mean he has to invite all of them."

She shrugged. "I don't know, but what I do know is that this wedding has to be fucking perfect, okay? I'm the kind of girl who won't have a big wedding because I truly don't give a fuck about most people, or about pleasing them, for that matter, but for other people, I *love* doing shit like this. Besides, you don't need the stress of it on top of college work." I smiled as she walked across my bedroom and capped my shoulders. "It won't be too big. It'll be chill and a night to remember. I promise, you have nothing to worry about."

"Fine," I laughed. "But no crazy stuff, like flame throwers and animals and performers. Simplicity is best."

"Deal!" She snatched me toward her, pulling me in for a hug. "I'm telling you. You won't regret it. I'll make it the best day ever!"

I was sure she would. We went downstairs to the den, where the sixty-inch TV was already primed for Netflix. Lora picked a movie that had Noah Centenio, her latest boy-crush, and then she pulled her phone out, going straight to Pinterest to show me some ideas she'd saved for us to discuss.

I never took Lora for the type to get excited about a wedding, but she was. She showed me dresses that she thought would look good on my frame and even color schemes and backdrops she assumed I would like. With everything I'd been shown, I had no doubt Lora was going to make this wedding epic. She was persistent and had very good fashion sense, but I didn't know how Cane would feel about her taking over every detail.

He'd told me he wasn't interested in a big wedding either. He wanted it to be quiet and private, with only people he really cared about there. Everyone he cared about was either under his roof or back in Georgia, but even I knew he was going to have to invite some of the people from work to his wedding, just to keep up appearances.

Still, the fact that we were getting married topped all of those worries. I was going to be a wife—and not just any wife. *His* wife.

CHAPTER 2

ANDY

MY PHONE BUZZED EARLY the next morning, and I groaned, reaching blindly for the nightstand.

When I felt it, I snatched it up, rolling over to answer it. "Hello?"

"Kandy?" Cane said. "You still sleeping?"

"Mm-hmm. Why?" I croaked. Ugh, I needed water.

"It's noon," he said, laughing a little. "You're usually awake by now."

"What?" I sat up, peering around the room.

"What did you do last night? Get drunk with Lora?" he joked.

"No, I didn't do anything. We watched a movie, and I went to bed early." I smelled something cooking and twisted my legs, dangling them over the edge of the bed. "Ugh—oh my God! What is that smell?" I covered my nose, pushing to a stand. "It smells like someone vomited all over the house."

"How is that possible? It's cleaning day," Cane said. "The housekeeper should have been there and done by now."

"I don't know, but it smells awful."

He laughed. "So maybe you *did* party last night. Sure there isn't vomit on that expensive bed of ours?"

I looked back, pushing a hand through my hair. "No," I moaned.

"Well, I'm about to head to the airport to catch my flight home. Just wanted to let you know in case you tried to get in touch. Mama told me she's making some kind of pasta tonight. I'll bring some wine with me."

"Okay, yeah. That sounds good."

"Love you, party girl."

I laughed. "I love you too. See you soon."

I sat on the bed and looked out of the window, covering my nose again. Why did it smell so bad in here? I couldn't remember the house ever smelling this way. Someone knocked on the door, and I went to answer it.

"Hey," Lora greeted when I opened it. "You finally awake, sleepyhead? I came up earlier to see if you wanted breakfast, but you were still sleeping."

"Ugh, yeah, I'm up." I sighed, clutching the doorknob. My arm slipped, and I stumbled a bit, but she caught me, steadying me by the arm.

"Whoa, Kandy. You feeling okay?" Lora asked, worry creasing at her forehead. "You don't look too good."

"Does something smell weird to you? D-did you throw up recently?" I tried to hold my breath.

She frowned. "What? No. What are you talking about?"

I heaved, and she gasped, holding my upper arms.

"Oh, God." I cupped my mouth, snatching away from her and rushing to my bathroom.

"Kandy?" she called after me, concern lacing in her voice, but I could hardly hear her over my own gagging. I dropped to my knees and clutched the porcelain of the toilet, letting out whatever was barely in my stomach.

"Jesus, are you okay?" She pulled my hair back, but I heaved again, feeling the burn in my throat.

"I must have eaten something bad yesterday." I wiped my mouth with the back of my arm, then dropped on my bottom on the floor, pressing my back to the cabinet behind me.

"First you say everything smells like vomit, and then you actually end up vomiting..." Lora's eyebrows pulled together. She tucked her fiery-orange hair behind her ears and dropped down to sit beside me. She was quiet for a moment, then looked sideways at me. "This feels familiar."

"What do you mean?"

"I mean, this has happened to me before."

My brows dipped. "Well, yes, Lora, I'm sure you have been sick before."

She sighed and got up to grab a washcloth, running it under cool water before she handed it to me. I wiped my face with it as she sat again.

"Kandy, I think we should go to the pharmacy for a pregnancy test."

My eyes nearly bulged out of my head. "What? Why would I do that?"

"Because I think you might be *pregnant*, Kandy," she said, laughing hoarsely. "I was expecting once, okay? And I remember that everything smelled like shit, and I could not stop vomiting or feeling dizzy."

"B-but I can't be. I—can't have kids. My doctor said it would be near impossible."

"Yeah...Cane told me about that." Her eyes dropped, but I tried to catch them.

"He did?"

"He was drunk when he admitted it. He kind of slipped up."

"Oh." I lowered my head.

"It was before Kelly died. That's why I *really* asked Jefe for the favor. Because she took something from you that no woman should ever have to live without." Her eyes locked on mine. "The right to be a mother."

Her words, although intense, warmed my heart. I loved that Lora cared, but I still hated how Kelly went, even though I hated that woman more than anyone. If I was pregnant, I was pretty sure she was flipping in her grave. "I accepted the situation a long time ago, Lora," I murmured with a shrug. "Maybe not before Kelly died, but I didn't need her dead to come to terms with it."

"Yeah, well, you shouldn't have had to. You deserve so much, Kandy." She grunted as she stood again. "If you're feeling sick, this is a good sign. It means that maybe something's happening in there and that all hope isn't lost. Let's get the test, see what it says. If it's positive, you'll have something special to tell Cane tonight."

"What?" I grabbed her hand before she could walk off. "No, Lora. We can't tell Cane until I know for sure that I don't lose it. My doctor said that even if I became pregnant, it could result in a miscarriage." My vision blurred as I looked her over. "And if I do lose it, I don't want him to witness it or know about it. I don't want him to feel like he has to take this on his shoulders after everything he's been through already."

She looked me over and I could tell she thought I was wrong for wanting to keep it a secret, but eventually she nodded. "Okay. Fine. I won't say anything if you don't want me to."

I'd kept a secret of hers before. I knew she'd keep mine, too. Of course, it wasn't right to withhold this kind of information from my own fiancé, but I didn't want to get my hopes up too soon, or his either. For all I knew, I just had food poisoning or a virus. And even if I was pregnant, I didn't want him to get excited, only for something terrible to occur.

I looked down at the cushion-cut diamond on my ring finger, remembering what all it stood for the night he'd proposed.

"Everything you go through, I'll be here for you. As long as you

promise to communicate with me, and to not keep me in the dark, we will get through it. No matter what it is," Cane said, looking me in the eyes as he slid the ring onto my finger. *It was a perfect fit. He was still on one knee, giving me his all.*

"And the same goes for you," I murmured, looking from the ring and into his eyes. "As long as you communicate with me, I'll always be here for you. No secrets. No lies."

He smiled, leaning up to kiss me on the lips. "You like the ring?" he asked when our lips parted.

I huffed a laugh, holding my hand up and staring at it. "I love it, babe." I dropped my arms, throwing them around the back of his neck. "I love it so much."

After so many years of struggling and almost losing everything, he didn't deserve to be put through another loss. I knew telling him was the wiser thing to do, but for the sake of his peace, I wanted to be sure before I said anything. I couldn't afford to ruin our happiness again.

CHAPTER 3

ANE

"What do you mean there's not enough fuel?" I was standing in front of my private jet, focused on my pilot, who was, unfortunately, getting the bitter end of my attitude. All I wanted was to get home, take a shower, and relax. I'd had a long few weeks, working with new clients for new franchises. I needed a damn break.

"I apologize for the inconvenience, sir," said Blake, my pilot. "I arrived here two hours before your arrival, like I always do. I spoke to those guys over there, and they told me they'd just used the last of what they had on two other jets." He pointed to the orange-vested men gathered around a work station. "They said there would be more delivered in a few hours, so as soon as they fill the jet, I can call it in and make a new plan for flight."

I shoved a hand to my hip and pinched the bridge of my nose with the other hand. "This is unbelievable. They knew my flight was happening, and they didn't think to order more fuel?"

"I'm sorry, sir. If you'd like, you can wait on board. It shouldn't be more than a few hours. The Wi-Fi is on, and the flight attendant has drinks ready."

I pressed my lips. "It's fine," I sighed. "It's not your fault. I'll wait on board, but keep me updated."

"Will do, sir."

I turned away from Blake, going up the stairs to get on the jet. As I boarded, I spotted the flight attendant standing by the mini bar to my right. "Good afternoon, Mr. Cane. Would you like me to make your favorite?"

"No. A little too early for scotch. Thanks, though."

With a grunt, I sat down, pulling out my laptop and cellphone. I decided to give Kandy another call, but there was no answer. I placed the phone down, frowning. She was acting strange this morning, and it wasn't like her *not* to answer my calls, no matter what she was doing. I assumed she was busy. Probably taking a shower or eating—something of that nature. She was going to be starting her senior year in about two weeks, so she could have been preparing for that.

Ever since I'd proposed to her, things had shifted. I could tell she was happy, but even I knew that deep down, more would change for her. Not only that, but she still hadn't told her parents yet. She wasn't sure how to break the news to them, especially with Derek. She knew Derek wasn't keen with having me around, but being engaged and then *married* meant I wasn't going anywhere, and he would have to deal with it.

I had no doubts about asking for her hand in marriage. I wanted her around for the rest of my life and didn't want her getting away from me again.

The time we spent in Belize was refreshing and exciting, not to mention we fucked a lot. I'd even found new trigger spots of hers that made her roll with orgasms. During that trip, I didn't work at all. I dedicated all of my time to her, and fell even more in love with that girl. I'd bought the ring three months prior to Belize, after all. I carried that velvet box with me, feeling the weight of it in my pocket every single day, waiting for the perfect moment to ask. When it finally came, I went for it, and I had no regrets.

THREE HOURS LATER, the jet was fueled up, and Blake announced that he was ready for takeoff. I closed my laptop and buckled in, but just as I was about to turn my cellphone off, a number popped up on my screen. I didn't know who it was, so I ignored it, but they called again. I ignored it once more. Then the same number sent a text message, and when I read over it, I couldn't believe who it was from.

Mr. Cane, This is Eden St. Claire. It would be wise to answer the phone when your new sponsor calls.

What the hell?

Just when I thought my life was getting easier, a message from *her* shows up. Now, out of all times. Now, when my life was just starting to turn around. Of course there was a storm coming. We'd had too much bliss, and it was due time, but what in the living fuck could Eden St. Claire want?

CHAPTER 4

KANDY

"THIS IS FUCKING INSANE," I huffed, sitting on the counter. Lora was standing beside me, reading over the instructions of the pregnancy test.

"It's really fucking simple, Kandy Jennings. Just pee on the stick."

"I don't mean that—I just mean, all of this." She peered up, and I focused on her eyes. "The doctor told me I had an 85 percent chance of not carrying a child. I don't want to take this test and be disappointed."

Her gray eyes shimmered as she studied mine. She then blinked quickly, taking a step back and sighing. "Look, Kandy…I understand why you're afraid. I would be, too, but you can't let that fear stop you from dealing with the situation. You're going to hate me for saying this, but I really think you should tell Cane now. He'd find you the best doctor in town to make sure you don't lose the baby."

"*If* there is a baby," I corrected, "and even so, that's my point. Cane has overbearing tendencies. If he knows, he won't rest until he's spent every dollar and sought every option possible to make sure this works out." I ran a hand over my stomach, lowering my gaze. "I don't want to put him through that."

"Well, you have to tell someone else you trust, Kandy. Someone who can get you an appointment with a good doctor, who will give you good advice and protect that little bean."

There was only one person who came to mind that I knew wouldn't judge me but would move heaven and earth if she knew there was a fighting chance for me to have a normal future. My eyes shifted over to my cellphone beside me and I picked it up, exhaling.

"There's only one person I can think of."

"Who?" Lora asked.

"My mom."

"Well, call her! Moms like to help. But first," she said, ripping the plastic of the pregnancy test open, "piss on the stick so we aren't jumping to conclusions."

I jumped off the counter, and she handed it to me. She turned for the door and closed it behind her, and I glared at the stick, as if it were a foreign object I'd never seen or heard of.

Walking to the toilet, I lifted the lid. Deep inside me, I knew something was going on. After I thought about it, I realized I'd had a collection of odd symptoms for a while. I was sluggish, fatigued, and everything smelled horrible. Not to mention my boobs started aching really bad last week, but I thought it was because my period was about to come on.

It was best to get this over with.

I pushed my pants and panties down, then squatted over the toilet. My body resisted the urge to pee, probably sensing the stick and refusing to give it an answer. I closed my eyes and breathed, and finally did what I had to do, capped the end and placed the stick on top of the commode. I flushed and waited.

And waited.

And waited some more.

When I took a peek, I couldn't believe what I saw. Two pink lines. So bold and absolutely clear.

"Holy fucking shit!" I screamed.

"What?" Lora's voice was loud, and she pushed the door open, barging into the bathroom. She rushed to my side, but I couldn't stop staring at the stick, and when she noticed too, she gasped and hugged my shoulders, hopping up and down a little. "Holy fucking shit is right! Bitch, you're pregnant!"

CHAPTER 5

ANDY

I TRIED NOT to freak out as I washed my hands and then grabbed my phone. I needed to call Mom. I didn't know how to handle this.

"I'll give you some space. Call me if you need me," Lora said, walking out the door, but she didn't get away without me noticing the big grin on her face. She was excited, but I was nervous as hell.

I watched her go and then went to Mom's name in my contact favorites. Pressing the phone to my ear, the ringing only increased my anticipation, and when she finally answered, I felt my heart drop to my stomach. A part of me kind of wished she hadn't answered.

"Kandy?" Mom answered.

"Hey, Mom."

"Hi, baby. How are you doing?" She sounded so calm. I hated that I had news that was definitely going to disturb her peace.

"I'm good. I just wanted to call and say hello..." *Hello? Seriously? When did I ever say that?* I slapped a hand to my forehead. *So stupid.*

"Oh, well, hi, sweetie," she laughed. "Everything okay? You normally don't call just to say *hello*."

"I know. Are you busy right now?"

"Sorta-kinda. I'm in the break room, making a few copies for a coworker of mine. What's going on?"

I paused, chewing on my bottom lip. "If I tell you something, you promise not to freak out about it?"

"It depends on what it is," she responded honestly.

"Just...promise that you won't."

"Okay." She sighed. "I promise. Now, what is it?"

"Well, Lora took me to a pharmacy, and we grabbed a pregnancy test—"

"Wait...WHAT?"

"Just listen," I said, holding up a hand, for all the good it did me. "I took it, and it came out positive, so I think I'm...pregnant."

She was quiet for a while, and my heart banged in my chest as I waited for her to say something—anything.

"By Cane?" Her voice was way too quiet.

"Yes, Mom. Of course Cane. Who else?"

"Were you not protecting yourself?"

"I didn't see the point, seeing as I had only a 15% chance of getting pregnant and all."

"I told you 15% was still a big number, Kandy! It's always smart to protect yourself, doesn't matter what the odds are."

I pinched the bridge of my nose. "Mom, I didn't call to get scolded, okay? I called because I want you to help me. I haven't told Cane yet, and I want to make sure I'm okay and that everything else is too, you know?"

"Why haven't you told him?"

"Because I'm worried it could be a false alarm. What if I miscarry? Then what?"

"Have you bled during the past few weeks?"

"No—none. I mean, I had my period a week after Belize, but since then, nothing." When she asked that, I don't even know why I didn't realize my period hadn't come on last month. Then again, since the stabbing, my periods had become very irregular.

"Well, that's a good sign. When do you think it might have happened? Conception?"

"It's hard to say…" My face felt hot. I might be a grownup, and a potential mother, but I did *not* feel comfortable talking to her about having sex with Cane, my much older fiancé and formerly a close friend of hers.

She lightly cleared her throat. "I can help you, sweetie, but you'll have to come here. I want to take you to Dr. Bhandari again, see what he can tell us. I'll call today and schedule an appointment."

"Okay, that sounds good."

"I'll text you and let you know when he'll have us. I'll tell him it's urgent. Anything could happen. In the meantime, don't move too much. Try to relax."

"Okay. I'll try." I walked toward the window, focusing on the line of trees. "Mom, do me a big favor and don't tell Dad."

"Trust me," she breathed, "I don't plan on telling him right now, but if there is hope, you'll have to tell him, Kandy. You can't hide a whole baby from him."

"I know." I dropped my gaze. "There's also something else you should know about Cane and me…"

"Oh, geez, Kandy! Really? What now?"

"When we went to Belize for our little getaway, he proposed to me…and I said yes."

"Oh, wow." She sounded both concerned and excited. I don't know how that was possible, but her tone couldn't fool me. She was happy for me, but also unsure about the idea of that. "The proposal must have been beautiful."

I grinned. "It was."

"Wasn't that trip like two months ago?"

"Yes," I answered feebly.

"And you're just *now* telling me?" I could sense the agitation in her voice now. "Kandy, why do you hide stuff like that from me? I'm your mother, sweetie. I deserve to know when my only daughter has gotten engaged."

"Yeah, I know, but if I'd told you, you would need to tell Dad, and I didn't want him to find out so soon. Not until we got closer to the wedding date, at least."

"And when might this wedding be?"

"Probably after I graduate…but if I am pregnant and nothing bad happens, it'll have to be when the baby is a few months old."

"Right." I heard her inhale deeply before exhaling. "Wow, sweetie, you have so much going on, but it's a good thing that *something* can happen for you. I still think you're too young for a kid, but it makes me happy to know there is a chance. I'll call you about Dr. Bhandari. I'll get the soonest date I can."

"Okay, Mom. Thanks."

"Of course, baby. Remember what I said. No strenuous stuff and no sex…please," she begged. "Sex is a trigger, and if you are pregnant and just a few weeks in, that's the last thing you want to do at such a high risk."

I nodded like she could see me. "I won't. I promise."

"And Kandy?"

"Yes?"

"Don't hide anything else from me, okay? I'm here for you, and you don't have to worry about me telling your father anything. I, of all people, know how he is. I know what to tell him and what to keep quiet about."

I smiled. "Okay. I won't hide anything else, I swear. Thank you for understanding, Mom."

"Of course. Love you, honey."

"Love you too."

I hung up and pushed my phone into my back pocket. I really hoped Mom could get the soonest appointment possible.

Knowing that there was a possibility that I could hold onto this baby meant the world to me. I didn't want to lose it, so I took her advice to heart and rested for the rest of the day.

I read on my Kindle, watched movies, and sipped on water, because none of the food or smoothies was doing it for me. Everything smelled horrible. The only kind of activity I did was run to the toilet every hour to empty my stomach. Lora came back up several times to check on me and to grin about the idea of becoming an aunt and Cane being a dad. It was adorable, really.

I kept wondering when conception might have happened, and there was one night that stood out in my mind, when Cane had come home from a work trip, and I was feeling extra frisky. It was about two weeks after Belize, and neither Lora or Mrs. Cane were home. Cane came up to the room, and the first thing I did was help him out of his clothes. From that moment on, we couldn't be stopped…and of course he didn't pull out. He hardly ever did anymore. I guess he assumed we were safe, after spending so many years together and me not ending up pregnant.

Perhaps we thought wrong.

CHAPTER 6

ANE

HELL NO, I wasn't calling Eden back.

To be frank, I never wanted to hear from that woman again after I left college. As soon as I was off my flight, I hopped into my car and had Neo take me home. Of course my phone rang again during the ride. One thing I remembered about that woman was her persistence. I knew she wouldn't stop calling, even when I got home, and the last thing I wanted to talk about with Kandy after not seeing her for three days was another woman calling me.

I groaned, head shaking as I lifted the phone. How in the hell did this happen? How was she a sponsor for Tempt, and I didn't know it? With a sigh, I finally answered.

"Eden," I answered coolly.

"He lives," she chimed, and I could hear the amusement in her voice. Already, she was getting a kick out of this.

"How did you get my number?"

"Oh, I have all of my clients' numbers."

"Client?" I questioned. "Since when did I become *your* client? I don't recall signing any deals with an Eden St. Claire."

"That's because you didn't."

"Explain now, before I hang up."

"Oh, boy. Still so harsh." She made a *tisk* noise. "Well, you may recall meeting a Gerald Miller?"

"Yes. He owns Paradise Golf Club."

"Well, I take care of the ground work for Mr. Miller's sponsorships. He invested a great deal into one of your Tempt stores in Charlotte, correct? I'm the woman who comes out to make sure our sponsorship banners, wording, and liabilities are correct."

Shit. I did not see that coming.

"I'm also the one who gets to decide if a sponsorship continues after twelve months or dies. Tempt already doesn't seem like it will be worth our time later."

"Is that a threat?"

"Oh, no. No threats, love. Mr. Miller is very interested in having his club endorse the Tempt brand. I also hear you have a shipment coming in for the club—free bottles of wine for our members. Great way to rope him in." She laughed. "You were always good at that."

"Eden, what the hell do you want?"

"I just wanted to inform you that I take my job seriously. When I come to Charlotte, I like to see our banners in a spot that many others can see, even from a distance. We will not have our name hidden in corners, or in the dark. We want to be where everyone can see us, so they know that our club is the place to go. I'll be arriving this Friday. I'd like to schedule a sit-down meeting with you to go over some paperwork."

"Then call my office and speak with my assistant. She handles my schedule."

"No, Cane, I don't think you're listening to me." Her voice was tighter. "I am coming on Friday and will be showing up at your office at ten in the morning, with my paperwork for you to sign.

No sooner, no later. See, the thing about my position is that I can yank this sponsorship away from you so easily that it'll be gone before you close your fist around it. I can make you look like a fool to Mr. Miller, just like you made me look."

My fist clenched in my lap.

"Friday at ten. If you have me wait, I will leave and let him know you weren't willing to work fairly with us."

"You do realize that Mr. Miller came directly to me and asked to be a sponsor? Though we can utilize the money, it's not like I begged for it."

"Yes, I realize that, but let's just say that Mr. Miller has a lot of pride and is very easy man to tick off. If I tell him you weren't willing to take a moment to sit down with me in regard to his club and all his sponsorship entails, he won't be a happy man, and he won't be quiet about it. The negative buzz will spread like wildfire."

"I don't like your tone," I hissed.

"And ever since my sophomore year in college, I don't like you, so I guess we're even."

I breathed hard through my nose. Neo was pulling up to my house, and I was sick of this bitch.

"Don't get too arrogant, Eden. You work for Mr. Miller, but I've played golf with him, so if he finds out you're making threats, I don't think he'd be too happy about that. You sound very confident that he'll take your word over mine. Why is that?"

"Because," she said, "Mr. Miller happens to be my *father*, and I'm the one who helped him expand this company with my sponsoring skills. I tell him where to promote himself and his club. He gets paid."

Of fucking course.

"Friday at ten," I snapped. "Now get the hell off my phone."

I hung up before she could say anything else to piss me off. It was just my luck that a former fling of mine was the daughter of a man who'd invested a great deal of money into Tempt. Tempt was doing fine, but his sponsorship was going to help us bring in dozens of jobs and internships. Having Eden fuck with that opportunity to expand my business really pissed me the fuck off.

"We're here, sir," Neo announced. "Should I get your bags?"

"No, Neo. It's fine. I'll grab them. Get back to your family. I'll see you this weekend."

"Yes, sir."

I pushed out of the car, tucking my phone into my pocket. I went for the trunk, took my suitcases out, walked to the house, and unlocked the front door. I heard some murmuring coming from the kitchen, and then laughter.

Placing my suitcase down, I headed down the hallway, following the sound. Mama and Lora were there. Lora had her elbows planted on the island counter, bent over a salad she was eating, and Mama was sipping something from a black mug.

"Look who's home!" Lora said in the same sarcastic way she always did.

I walked up to them, giving them quick hugs. "Where's Kandy?"

"Upstairs. She's not feeling too good today," Mama stated.

"Stomach bug, probably," Lora filled in rapidly, putting on a small smile.

"Hmm. She been like that all day?"

"Since this morning," Lora shrugged.

"Let me check on her." I turned and made my way upstairs and to the bedroom. Kandy was on the bed, her hair sprawled all over the place. She was sound asleep, and it was only 8:30 at night. *Didn't she sleep in this morning?*

Sighing, I sat on the edge of the bed, close to her, and pushed her hair back. She moaned a little, rustled around a bit. She looked like she was sleeping so peacefully. As badly as I wanted to tell her about that dreaded phone call I just had, I didn't want to disturb her rest. I pulled the comforter on top of her, then kissed her cheek.

Going to the closet, I changed into something more comfortable, but when I came back out, Kandy's eyes were halfway open.

"Cane?" she groaned.

"Yeah, babe. It's me." I climbed onto the bed, pulling her to my chest as she moaned. "Lora says you have a stomach bug."

She yawned. "Oh. Yeah...something like that."

"Feeling any better?" I glanced at the ginger ale on her nightstand.

"Still feeling a little sick."

"Need me to get anything?"

"No." She hugged me tight, nuzzling her cheek into my chest. "I just need you. That's all."

I smiled, stroking her hair back. That phone call may have had me on edge, but being with her and having her arms wrapped around me took some of the edge off. I wanted to tell her what was going on—I'd promised her no more secrets—but right now wasn't the time. Not while she was sick.

I told myself I'd fill her in once she felt better. Eden's presence wasn't to be taken lightly. I remembered a lot about her, and one thing I knew for sure was that she was going to make my life a living hell after what I'd done to her. It was best to brace myself, because until my contract with Mr. Miller was up, I wasn't going to see or hear the end of that wicked woman.

Too bad the contract wouldn't be up for another three hundred or so days, and I, of all people, knew how much shit could change in the span of a year.

CHAPTER 7

ANDY

I THOUGHT I'd feel better after a few days, but I was so, so wrong. If anything, I felt worse. I was sick to my stomach constantly. Mom said the soonest she could get an appointment with Dr. Bhandari was on Thursday, and I was so ready for that day. I guess it was a good sign that all of this was happening, though. It meant my body was doing something right, or progressing at least, in preparation for a little one.

Mom wasn't wrong, though—I was just getting started in life, and having a baby was going to throw me for a really big loop. It was hard to even worry about that, though, given that the odds were still so against me.

For the next three days, I walked around like a zombie, trying to keep up appearances for Cane, but it wasn't working, and I was sure he was starting to notice. He kept asking if I was okay, or why I wasn't eating much. And the smell of his cologne was starting to annoy me. For the first time, I wished he was working out of town so he wouldn't be here paying attention, and I wouldn't have to sneak and run upstairs, just so he wouldn't hear me throwing my guts up.

Either way, he seemed preoccupied with his own work issues, which helped. He went to the office every day from 8:00 a.m. to 7:00 p.m., and even came home with work to do sometimes, so it kept him occupied for the most part.

When Wednesday rolled around, I waited up for him instead of falling asleep like I had been. He got home around 8:00 p.m., and when I heard him coming upstairs, I sat up a little higher in the bed, pressing my back to the headboard.

"Oh, you're up," he greeted with a smile. He walked around the bed, dropping a kiss on my forehead. "Still not feeling well?"

"I'm better," I lied. "I stayed up because I wanted to tell you that I'm driving to Atlanta tomorrow to meet Mom for lunch. I haven't seen her in a few months. Kinda miss her."

"Is that why you've been moping around lately?" he asked, focusing on my eyes. "If so, you should go—get out of the house. You don't have to ask me to visit your parents, babe," he said, untying his tie. "You can go whenever you want. I understand."

"I know, I just wanted you to know. I'll probably be back tomorrow night. Just a quick trip to see what they're up to."

"I'm all for it. Need anything?"

"No. I still have money on the credit card for gas and whatever else." I climbed off the bed and walked up to him. "You seem bothered," I mentioned, because he did, but he always got like this when he was stressed out about something that involved work. One thing about Cane was that he kept work issues at work and didn't bring them into our home life if he could avoid it.

He lowered his gaze, lips pressing together. "I'm a little stressed, but I'll deal with it." He caressed my cheek. "You, on the other hand, are the one who seems a little out of sorts. You sure you're okay?"

"I'm fine. Promise." God, I hated lying to him. He deserved the truth, but I wasn't ready to tell him just yet. I wanted to hear what Dr. Bhandari had to say before making any sort of announcement. "I think I need to see my mom. Catch up a little bit." I grabbed his hand and made him sit on the edge of the bed. I climbed up behind him, placing my hands on his shoulders and starting a massage. "Will this help you relax?" I asked, rubbing his shoulders with the pads of my fingers.

"Oh, yeah," he sighed. "It's helping."

"You sure everything is okay, Cane?" I couldn't help thinking we were both holding back on something.

He reached up for my hand, looking over his shoulder. "Come here," he murmured. He turned a little, bringing me onto his lap. I wrapped my arm around the back of his neck, and he let out a weary breath, holding me snug to his body.

"There is something you should know about work," he began.

"What is it?"

He looked me in the eyes very briefly before looking away. "There is a woman I have to work with because of a sponsorship. Eden St. Claire."

"Okay?" I sat up, pulling my arm from the back of his neck. A woman? "What about her?"

"She and I went to college together. We fooled around back then, but it didn't get very far. She was too…*ridiculous* for me."

I swallowed hard. "Ridiculous? What do you mean? Why are you telling me this?"

"Because I did something to her that she's holding a grudge about. If I'd known she was in charge of the sponsorships for the golf club we just took on, I wouldn't have signed the contract. She's making threats, Kandy, and she's going to try and play mind games with me until the contract is up. She'll make work a living hell."

"Well, when is the contract up?"

"It's in effect for a year."

"Jesus, Cane. A year." I climbed off his lap, standing in front of him.

"The only reason I haven't found a way to terminate my contract with them is because this is a big deal for Tempt. Her father gave us enough money to salary out several great employees and fund a bunch of internships. One of my dreams is to help people, Kandy. Give them something to do—something to look forward to every day. I want Tempt to be the place that allows miracles and chances."

"I understand that, Cane, but can you not work with someone else for the sponsorship? Maybe tell them you're not comfortable working with her one-on-one?"

"I've tried, Kandy. She's head of that department. Has nothing more than an assistant. Not to mention she's the owner's daughter." He dropped his head while my eyes expanded. "She'll be here Friday for paperwork. I already know she's going to try and ruin shit, but I'm telling you now so you don't panic or think something crazy is going on, because it isn't and never will be."

"You seem really anxious. What did you do to her?"

He looked away from me completely and paused, inhaling through his nostrils and then back out. "When we were in college, she had this crazy libido. She kept asking me to do things with her that I didn't like doing. She asked me to take part in a threesome, an orgy—all this crazy shit, but I never did. I was getting fed up with her requests because I felt boring, you know? Like I wasn't good enough. She apologized about it one day, said she would calm down, and then said she'd make it up to me by taking me on a ski trip. She begged me to go, so I caved and said I would." He finally met my eyes. "She'd booked flight tickets, a cabin, and everything, but I just couldn't do it. I stood her up. Left her waiting at the airport."

"Oh my gosh, Cane! Of course she's going to make your life a living hell! Why would you stand her up?"

"I was young, okay? I knew she wasn't the woman for me; I

35

didn't like her like that. We were just having fun at first, but when I realized how serious she was, it was a turn off. I didn't want a woman who craved four cocks at once. I wanted a woman who only wanted *me*, and she wasn't that person."

I felt my face relax and looked him all over. Well, I guess I couldn't blame him for that, but if I were in her shoes, I'd have been devastated, too— and looking for revenge. "Aww...Cane." I walked back up to him, lacing my arms around the back of his neck again.

"No man wants to feel like they aren't enough," he went on. "I knew I could be more than enough for someone else one day, so I moved on. Was it fucked up? Yes. But I was an asshole back then who refused to face her. I apologized through email like a fucking punk."

My lips smashed together. I rested my cheek on his chest, closing my eyes with a steady sigh. "I understand," I whispered.

"Are you upset?"

"No." How could I be upset, anyway? It was long before I was a part of his life .

He brought his hands up to cup my face and leaned back just enough to look into my eyes. "Are you worried?"

"A little. She sounds like a seductive person. Even her name is sexy." I laughed dryly.

"I'm hoping she's not like that anymore...but even if she is, you don't have to worry about that, okay? I love *you*. You are my future wife, and I would never do anything to betray you." He planted a kiss on my lips, and despite my nausea, I felt a puddle of heat deep in my core. "You trust me?"

I nodded slowly. "I trust you."

"Good." He kissed me again then dropped his arms to hold me. It wouldn't have been like Cane to not have more baggage. He'd dated many women in the past. There was bound to be at least another who would come for him, especially with how wealthy and powerful he'd become over the years. Besides, this Eden sounded like a breeze in comparison to the tornado that was Kelly Hugo.

I rested my head on his shoulder, drawing in a deep breath. He'd told me what was bothering him, yet I'd still kept my mouth shut. Right now was the perfect opportunity to spill...but I couldn't. Not yet. The guilt was real, and it was eating me alive. I couldn't wait to go to the doctor and get results. Then I could tell him, and everything would go back to the way they used to be.

CHAPTER 8

KANDY

My drive to Atlanta went by much slower than I'd hoped, most likely because I was anxious to know what would happen.

I really wanted there to be good news, but with my family's history, and what my body had suffered through because of what Kelly did to me, I knew my chances were slim. Still, I clung to hope.

I met Mom at a brunch cafe and left my car in the parking lot, riding with her the rest of the way to Dr. Bhandari's office.

"Is there a deeper reason why you haven't told Cane yet?" Mom asked when we neared the clinic.

I shifted in my seat, putting my focus on the street ahead. "I just don't want him to get too excited or nervous, or whatever he feels. He has a lot going on at work."

She scoffed. "When doesn't he?"

"I'm going to tell him. I just want to make sure that my chances aren't too low, you know?"

"Yeah." She tapped a finger on the steering wheel. "You think he'll be excited to know?"

"I don't know." I shrugged. "We've only talked about kids a few times—mostly when we were in Belize. I don't think he minds the idea of it anymore."

"Well, that's good to know." She rolled up to the clinic, parking in the lot. Shutting the car off, she asked, "You ready?"

I nodded and grabbed my satchel, getting out of the car with her. We walked into the clinic, where several women were already waiting. After checking in, it only took ten minutes for Dr. Bhandari's nurse to call us back. She checked my weight first, and I was surprised to see I'd gained seven pounds. After I left a urine sample, we were taken to the exam room, and the nurse did a blood pressure check, checked my pulse, and then informed me that Dr. Bhandari would be coming to see me at any moment.

"Good morning, Miss and Mrs. Jennings!" Bhandari sang, trotting into the room.

Mom and I smiled at his cheerful demeanor. "You're in a good mood," Mom noted.

"Oh, I am always in a good mood! I start my mornings with deep meditation. Gets me through the days, even the tough ones. But enough about that." His eyes swooped over to mine. "I hear that someone may be expecting!"

I laughed. "Yes."

"Well, I have your test results from your urine sample here, and if you had any doubts before about being pregnant, you can put those to rest because you are indeed expecting, Miss Jennings!"

"Really?" My heart seemed to beat harder and faster as I held my belly. "Do you think everything will be okay?"

"That is what I am going to find out right now. Do me a favor and lie back on the table for me. Let's see how everything is looking."

If I thought my heart was beating too fast before, it felt like it was going to pump out of my chest now. What if he checked and nothing was happening? What if something was wrong?

I laid back as he called the nurse in. She helped get me situated, feet in the sock-covered stirrups, and Dr. Bhandari went straight to work. He ran the wand of the ultrasound over my stomach, his eyes focused on the computer screen. "Ahh…there that little one is."

I stared at the screen, narrowing my eyes. I didn't see much of anything at first, just black and white spots, but then he clicked a button, and focused on one spot in particular.

"Do you see that?" he asked, pointing to a circular spot on the screen. "That is your baby, Miss Jennings." I gasped and looked over at Mom, who'd cupped her mouth. Dr. Bhandari kept moving the wand and clicking. "You know, I was looking at the last ultrasounds of your damaged uterus. It looks nothing like before."

"Seriously?" I asked. "How does it look now?"

He stopped moving the wand to focus on me. "Strong," he said with a smile. "Were you taking the vitamins I recommended?"

"Yes."

"They seem to have paid off for you! The embryo looks firmly attached there." He placed the wand down and picked up a clipboard. "Have you had any bleeding in the past few weeks?"

"No. None."

"That is great to hear, too."

"So are you saying her body will be okay for pregnancy?" Mom asked.

"I would say that she is very high risk. Although the embryo seems to be holding on and looks secured, there are a lot of variables at work here. I suggest visiting me or another preferred doctor every week. I'd still like to get some internal ultrasound images. Those can be a little more uncomfortable, but they will allow me to really see what is going on in there with the baby and the lining of your uterus."

"Sure. Anything," I breathed. My heart was fluttering so fast in my chest.

Dr. Bhandari got his images, but while I laid on that bed, all I could think about was what Cane would say when I told him. There was still a possibility of something bad happening, but maybe if I did exactly what they said and took it easy, it would be okay.

When we were done, Dr. Bhandari told us he'd send me his suggestions via email once he looked over the images, to determine what to do next. In the meantime, he'd given me some prenatal pills and a prescription for a nausea medicine.

Mom stopped by Panera for lunch, although I couldn't really down the food. It looked amazing, but the aromas were really making me want to barf. We didn't stay there for very long.

On the way back to my car, Mom said, "You know, even if something bad happens, which I pray it doesn't, I still think you should tell Cane. Those moments are hard, Kandy. You're going to need someone to help you pull through it. My someone was your father. If I hadn't had him, I don't know what I would have done."

I felt her eyes on me, but didn't bother meeting her eyes. I was too busy looking at my ultrasound pictures.

"Once we hear from Bhandari, I'll tell him," I told her, running my finger over the black and white image.

"Okay, sweetie."

When we got to the lot where my car was parked, Mom said she had to meet with a client to go over a case, and I didn't want to hold her up, so I hugged her tight and watched her go. During my drive, though, I got an email from Dr. Bhandari.

HELLO MISS JENNINGS,

I'M CONTACTING you in regard to your appointment with me

earlier. I just want to let you know that I was correct about the embryo being firmly attached. You look to be around five weeks along. As you are considered high risk, I suggest waiting to announce your pregnancy until at least the 8 week mark, when we can hear the baby's heartbeat. Around 13 weeks, the likelihood of a successful pregnancy increases exponentially. If you begin to cramp too much or even start spotting, please do not hesitate to seek help or call me. I can't say what will happen in the future, but I will say that there is always a fighting chance, if not now, then in the future. Make sure you take your prenatal vitamins. If there are any problems or cause for concern, please call. I hope to see you again in two weeks.

BEST REGARDS,

VIC BHANDARI

MY HEART SEEMED to drop to my stomach. He'd mentioned there was a fighting chance, but it didn't sound as promising as I hoped.

I drove the rest of the way home, trying to figure out what exactly to tell Cane. It wasn't like I could go up to him and act like I was in the clear. I still had eight more weeks before I could know for sure, and even so, that was a long time from now. Anything could happen.

When I got home, no one was there, and I was slightly relieved. I trudged up to my room and curled up beneath the comforter, glad that my nausea had subsided for the moment. I fell asleep, not waking again until around two in the morning. Cane was in bed with me, his arms thrown over his forehead, covering one of his eyes. He was snoring, which was rare. He must have been really tired.

The interesting thing about Cane's sleep habits now was that he slept more since I'd moved in. He didn't toss and turn like before. He literally slept like a baby.

And speaking of babies, I didn't even think about how much things would change by having one. Mom had told me so much, like how she had permanent bags under her eyes because I was a terrible sleeper as a baby and a kid. And also how she had to wear pantyliners every day for two years because when she sneezed, coughed, or laughed too hard, she'd leak a little.

Don't get me wrong—Mom still had a great body, but a lot had changed for her when she gave birth to me. Was I ready for that yet? For my entire world to shift? My body to change?

I rested on my back, staring up at the ceiling fan. I placed a flat hand on my belly and inhaled deeply before letting it go. If it was meant to be, I knew it would happen. If it wasn't, then I had to face that truth when it arrived...but Mom was right about what she said before. I couldn't do it alone. If things did go bad, I wanted him to be there for me.

This was our seed. We'd planted it together, and we'd deal with it the same way.

Together.

CHAPTER 9

Cane

I'D BEEN DREADING this morning all week long. I sat at my desk, sipping on the coffee a new intern had delivered, when Cora walked in. "Sir, she's here," she announced, worry swirling in her eyes.

I groaned, placing my cup down and pushing out of my chair. "Let's get this over with. Send her in."

With a nod, Cora took off. Several seconds later, there she was.

Eden St. Claire.

Don't get me wrong, Eden was a very good looking woman. She had smooth, topaz skin and had aged nicely. Her dark hair was straightened, reaching just past her shoulders, and large diamonds were in her ears. I'm certain with a father as rich as Gerald Miller, they were real diamonds. She was easy on the eyes—eye candy, as many men would say—but her inner flaws made her less than appealing.

"Eden," I bellowed, stepping around the desk and extending my arm to offer a hand.

"Mr. Cane," she said in response, grabbing my hand and shaking it. She looked deep into my eyes, a smirk on her lips. "You look great."

"As do you." I released her hand, gesturing to the chairs behind my desk. "Sit, please," I said, walking back to my chair. She sat first, and I placed my elbows on the desktop while she pulled a folder from under her arm.

She placed it on the desk and opened it, peering up at me beneath lashes that were caked with mascara. "You have more tattoos since college," she noted.

"I'd prefer that we not rehash past history. Let's keep this professional."

She paused, picking her head up to meet my eyes. "Do you really think I came all this way just to talk business? I mean, I knew you were a bit dim in college at times, but didn't realize it would carry over the years."

"Insulting me won't heal old wounds, Eden. Look, I apologize for what happened. Trust me, I wish I'd just told you that I wasn't going to go."

She fixed her jaw, lowering her head and flipping through the paperwork. "Honestly, these papers would have been so simple for me to scan and send for you to print and sign, but I wanted to see the look on your face when you saw me."

I sat back in my chair. "What did you think I would do? Get nervous?"

"Are you?" she challenged.

"Not at all."

Her tongue ran over her lips. "I hear you are engaged. When's the wedding."

"Next fall."

"Hmm." She smirked. "Let's hope you don't stand the bride up at the altar like you did me at the airport."

"Not going to happen." I held both hands out, as if the answer were right in front of us. "She's the love of my life."

Her eyes narrowed as she slid several sheets of paper across my desk. "Who is she, anyway? A lot of people have been wondering who this lucky lady is."

"Her name is none of your concern." I grabbed a pen, reading over the first sheet. I'd read them before, but I didn't trust Eden, and I wouldn't put it past her changing terms to make me look like a fool in the end. I signed it after reading it, and as I went to the next sheet, Eden stood and walked around the office.

"Are you ashamed of her?" she asked, looking out the window. "Like you were ashamed of me?"

"Why do you still hold onto that anger?" I questioned, frowning. "It was years ago. We were kids."

"Yes, but I *really* liked you, and you didn't even give me a fair chance."

My nostrils flared, and I shook my head, reading over the next page carefully before signing.

"As I recall," I murmured, "I gave you many fair chances. Shit happens. Most people learn to let it go. We weren't compatible."

"You weren't trying to be compatible," she spat, folding her arms. She looked me over in my chair. "You just thought you were better than me."

"That's far from true. I assumed I wasn't *enough* for you, and I let it go. Don't tell me you haven't met anyone after me? I'm certain you have."

"I have," she declared, coming closer to the desk. "And he was great. We were together for four years…but apparently I was too much for him too."

"There are men out there who desire the things you do. Maybe you're just choosing the wrong men."

She scoffed, and before I knew it, she was standing at the edge of my desk, only a few steps away from me. Her hand touched my shoulder, and I glared up at her. "Eden, you need to get your hands off of me and take a seat."

"God, I used to love that," she sighed. "Your bossiness. The possessiveness. I always knew you'd end up being your own boss one day."

I clenched my jaw. She started to move behind me but I pushed out of my chair, frowning. "Is this why you came? Because you think something will happen between us?"

She simply smiled. Nothing more.

"Okay, let me fill you in on something," I snapped, taking a step closer. "I love my fiancée. I've been in love with her for years, and it doesn't stop now, just because someone from my *past* comes knocking on the door. There is nothing between us, Eden, so just back off and do your damn job."

"Or what, Cane? You'll tell my father?" She gave me a smug smile. "Did you notice he and I don't have the same last names?" She looked me over. "Yeah, it's because he's a lying bastard who went behind his wife's back to sleep with a woman named Valerie St. Claire. My mother didn't think he was worthy to have a child named after him. His wife couldn't have kids, so of course she resents me for being a living, breathing creation of his. Every time I see her, I see the hate in her eyes, but you know what? I don't care, because I am his only child, and I have him wrapped around my finger, and she knows she'll never be able to get rid of me. My father already knows how I am. He knows that I like to take what I want; he's fine with it as long as I don't disrupt his plans."

I opened my mouth to retort, but there was a knock on my door. Cora popped her head in, and Eden stepped back, turning her back to us and looking out the windows again.

"Sir, your fiancée is here. She said she needs to speak with you."

I narrowed my eyes then looked over Cora's shoulder at Kandy, who was standing in front of Cora's desk with a small smile. She gave me a cute wave, but her eyes were full of worry. It wasn't like her to just show up without letting me know first. Something wasn't right.

"Send her in," I insisted, grabbing my pen and signing the final paper. "Miss St. Claire was just leaving." I stacked the papers to line them up then handed them to Eden with a dismissive glance. Cora walked back out, nodding and saying something to Kandy, and when Kandy came into the office, she rushed my way, throwing her arms around me. Her lips found mine along the way, and I kissed her back, groaning a little as she deepened it.

"Kandy?" I breathed. "What's wrong?"

"Nothing. I just have something to tell you. You left early this morning, so I didn't get the chance. Thought I would surprise you." Her eyes shifted over to Eden, who had walked up to the desk to collect the papers and put them back in her folder.

"Well, hello," Eden said to her, wearing that same smug smile she had on earlier. "I'm Eden St. Cl—"

"I know who you are," Kandy interrupted, giving her a frosty glare.

"Oh. You do?" Eden smiled, sliding her eyes over to me. "You've told her all about me, huh, Cane?"

"I don't keep secrets from her."

"Is that your thing now? Honesty? Gotta tell ya, it doesn't really fit you."

"You can leave now, Eden," I said as calmly as possible, wrapping my arm around Kandy's waist.

"Oh, don't worry. I was just going." She tucked the folder under her arm. She stopped a few steps away from us on the way out, putting her attention on Kandy. "I didn't catch your name," she said.

"It's Kandy."

"You are very young, Kandy." Eden smirked at me. "He'll definitely end up leaving you at the altar."

She trotted her way out, and Kandy watched her go until she could no longer see her. When Eden was nowhere in sight, Kandy turned to me with a grimace. "You didn't tell me she was *that* pretty!"

"What?" I hissed. "She doesn't look better than you, Kandy."

"Oh, please. Bullshit."

I walked around her, closing my office door. "I told you I had a meeting with her today. Is that why you showed up? I thought you trusted me." I stood in front of her, folding my arms.

"Get over yourself, Cane. That's not even why I'm here. To be honest, I completely forgot about the meeting with your nymphomaniac ex-girlfriend." She had that crease in her forehead, the one where I knew she was mad, but it made her look too damn cute and innocent to take seriously.

"What's wrong then?" I reached out, reeling her in by the waist.

"Is she going to be a problem?" she asked, pointing back with her thumb. "Because if she is, I want you to know that I'm not in the mood for it, okay? And what the hell did she mean *you'll be leaving me at the altar*? What kind of person says that?"

"Kandy, she is not going to be a problem, all right? She's just trying to get under your skin. That's it. She's still living in the past, but I'm moving forward. You have nothing to worry about."

She combed her fingers through her hair. "Okay...whatever. Look." She grabbed my hands and squeezed them. "I know you said we aren't supposed to keep secrets from each other, but there's something I have to tell you."

My brows pulled together. "What is it?"

Her throat bobbed, and with an exasperated breath, she dragged me to my chair and made me sit, then sat on my lap. "Okay, remember when I said was visiting my mom for lunch yesterday?"

"Yeah?"

"Well, we didn't just have lunch. She took me to see my gynecologist again."

"What? Why?" I asked.

"Because..." She bit her bottom lip. "Okay, here's the thing. I haven't been feeling well the past few days. It started big time a couple days ago, when you were out of town. Lora took me to get a pregnancy test, and when I took it...it came back positive." She looked me in the eyes, and I heard my pulse in my ears, slow and deep, as she said the words I never thought I would hear. "I'm pregnant, Cane."

CHAPTER 10

KANDY

"WAIT. WHAT!" His voice wasn't angry, but by the expression on his face—his wide eyes and slack jaw—I could tell he was surprised. Much more than I assumed he would be. "But...shit. How—I mean, don't get me wrong, I'm happy as fuck to hear this, but...*how?*"

"I don't know." I bubbled out a half-laugh, half-sob as I looked him in the eyes. "I just—I am!"

"Shit...baby. Holy fuck, this changes so much!" He collected me in his arms. "Are you glad?" he asked, stroking my hair back. "Excited?"

"I'm not sure how I feel yet. My doctor said my uterus is much better now. A lot stronger. The baby implanted well." I looked up at him. His eyes were glistening. Was he happy or upset about this? "I wanted to tell you days ago, but I wanted to hear from the doctor first. The thing is..." I pulled out of his arms and stood, grabbing his hands. "There's still a big chance that I could miscarry, Cane. Even though everything looks good for now, the doctor isn't making any promises."

"Bullshit. You have my baby inside you now, Kandy. *We* did that." He studied my eyes, his still damp. "Before, he told you there was barely a chance. Now you are and…" He sucked in a breath and smiled. "It's fucking incredible, baby. You're strong and resilient. We'll do whatever we need to do to make sure you and the baby are okay."

I have to admit, I was shocked to hear him saying all of this. I thought surely he'd need time to process the fact that he would become a father soon, but his smile…it was real. His words were real.

"Are you really happy about this?" I asked softly.

"Fuck, Kandy." He capped my shoulders and looked up at the ceiling briefly before leveling his eyes with mine again. "I'm starting a new life with you. Will a lot change for us with a baby? Yes, but this isn't something we can't handle. This is a chance, and we need to take it."

"But what if I do end up losing it?" I looked down at my stomach. "I'm scared that I will, Cane."

"No." He reeled me closer, dropping a kiss on the middle of my forehead. "You can't think like that."

"Dr. Bhandari said by thirteen weeks he'll have a much better idea of how my body is handling the pregnancy…if I make it that far."

"How many weeks along are you now?"

"He said five."

"Hmm. Not too long now. Two months." He leaned back to look at me. "I don't want you thinking negatively about this, all right? You've got me. I'm here, Kandy."

"I know." I tucked my hair behind my ears, walking around him to sit on the edge of his desk.

"Shit," he hissed, turning to face me with his hands on his hips.

"What?"

"Have you told your dad?"

"That...is something I have to think about. I have to figure out how to tell him without him flipping tables and slamming doors. I haven't even told him we're engaged yet."

"Fuck, he's really gonna kill me now." He huffed a laugh, stepping between my legs.

I grabbed his face, cupping it in my hands and leaning up just a bit to kiss him on the lips. When the kiss broke, I ran the tip of my nose over his and let our foreheads connect. "Are you sure you're happy with this?" I whispered. "I don't want to ruin what we have."

"I'm happy that it's possible." He lowered his hands to my waist. "Look, Kandy...the things I said to your dad years ago about having kids? That's in the past. I don't feel that way anymore. Being with you changed all of that. Having a kid gives me the chance to be a better man. Not only that, but imagine how cute the little thing would be." He put on a full, boyish smile, and I giggled, pressing a hand to his chest.

"He or she would be cute." I met his soft, gray-green eyes. "What do you want it to be? If we make it that far?"

He thought on it for a moment. "A boy, so he can look after you and protect you when I get too old to do so."

I couldn't fight my smile. All of this baby talk was making me emotional as hell, so instead of responding with words, I responded with action, and kissed my fiancé.

I was going to do everything in my power to carry this baby right and hope there wasn't a tragedy at the end. Cane and I deserved this. After everything we'd been through, we deserved our own slice of happiness. We'd faced a lot of battles, been through a lot of wars, but going through a high-risk pregnancy was going to be our biggest fight of all.

Deep in my heart, I knew it could either make us or break us. I prayed it would be the former.

CHAPTER 11

Cane

A BABY?

I still couldn't wrap my mind around it, yet the truth had been spilled, and I'd swallowed it all. She'd even shown me the ultrasound pictures. After so many years, I didn't think it was possible for us, yet there it was. She'd run straight to me with the possibility that maybe we could have a good life after all, with a family we created. I knew she really wanted a kid one day—or to at least try for one when she was ready.

I wouldn't have called this an accident, but rather a blessing in disguise. I just prayed this blessing lasted the full nine months.

Over the course of the next month, Kandy was anxious, while I was….*slightly* overbearing. As soon as she'd told me, I had Cora look into the best gynecologists in the metro area. I booked an appointment for her to be seen, and Mindy drove to Charlotte to tag along. She didn't want to miss out on any of the details.

For the most part, the doctor said Kandy was fine—the same

results her last doctor had uncovered. But Dr. Maxine suggested Kandy pretty much be on modified bedrest. She didn't have to stay in bed all day, but she wasn't supposed to stand more than a half hour at a time, and no strenuous working out, driving, or sex.

You'd think Kandy would have listened and taken things a little more seriously, but did she? No. She was so damn hardheaded, and I was getting fed up.

"Did you not hear what your doctor said, Kandy? You are not getting on that treadmill!" I was standing in front of the treadmill in her office, blocking her way.

"It's a harmless walk, Cane! I won't even go fast! I don't want to just sit around getting lazy and fat."

"It doesn't matter if you go fast or slow, you shouldn't be on it! You're supposed to be relaxing as much as possible!"

"Oh, my God, you are unbelievable!" She rushed around me to get out of the room, hurrying down the stairs. I rushed after her.

"Kandy, slow the hell down! You have slippers on! You could fall!"

"Yeah, well, if I fall, I'll just fucking fall, Cane!" She went down the hallway to get to the kitchen. When I got in there, she was yanking the fridge open, taking out a green smoothie. Mama was in the kitchen as well, looking between us, trying to figure out what was going on.

"What? Are you going to tell me I can't drink this, or it might poison the baby?"

I planted my hands above my hips. "Shit, will it?"

"Ugh." She rushed around the counter to get past me, glaring back once before disappearing.

"Slow your ass down!" I bellowed, but I was certain she didn't listen.

"Cane, you have to give her some space," Mama insisted.

"Space? What space? What if she falls or trips, then what? She could lose it all over a stumble!"

"I get that, but right now, she's hormonal, fatigued, nauseous, and stressed, and those four things combined are not a good feeling, son. And it's not good for the baby, either."

I sighed, sitting on the stool at the counter. Mama was frosting a red velvet cake. Apparently she was in charge of bringing baked treats to her sobriety meetings. She no longer attended as a person who needed to understand their wrongs, but more so as someone who coached others into wellness. She'd gotten into doing yoga and meditation, and I think it was paying off for her.

"Look, Ma, the doctor told her she needed to relax. I was there to hear it myself last week. She practically wants her on bedrest until the thirteen weeks are over. She's lucky I'm even letting her get out of the bed, let alone come down the stairs wearing those stupid slippers around the damn house! They don't even have traction on the bottom!"

Mama chuckled, head shaking.

"What's so funny?"

"You," she continued a light laugh. "I remember when everything she did was so cute to you. Now you're upset because she has a mind of her own, even stooping so low as to call her slippers *stupid.*"

I rolled my eyes, pulling out my cellphone when it chimed. "They are dumb. That fuzzy shit on them gets all over my bed." I read over the email from Eden and rolled my eyes a second time.

> **As you are aware, I wasn't pleased with the sponsorship banner your team created for the store.**
> **I'll be arriving Thursday morning to see the new one. I expect you to be there.**

"Look, I get that you want her and the baby to be safe, but she's dealing with a lot as it is," Mama said. "Maybe you can go for a walk with her in the neighborhood, get some air. I'm sure she's tired of being cooped up in this house, and if she gets the chance to see that baby's eyes one day, she'll get enough of being trapped in here anyway. Trust me, it's best if she gets out while she can. When is the baby due exactly?"

"They think around early April. The sixth of April is the precise date the doctor gave us." I groaned, rubbing my face. "I'm worried. That's all. I keep thinking about the downside of all of this, and I know it will haunt her. I've read about it, and miscarriages aren't easy. She said her mom went through them, so she'll have someone to talk to who understands, if it does happen, but I don't want her going through that. I just want her to be careful and to take this a little more seriously. I mean, I know she cares, but she's still young and naive about a lot of things."

"I know, baby, but you can't fight fate. If it's meant to happen, it will happen. Besides, she's young, and all young people think they're safe from harm until something bad happens—not saying that it will. But, you know." She shrugged. "That's one of the trials when it comes to being in a relationship that has an age difference, I suppose."

"I guess."

She finished icing the cake and then cut two slices, putting them on separate plates. "There. One for you, and one for Kandy." She cocked her head. "Get up there. Make up with her."

I sighed, picking up the plates and the forks and carrying it to our bedroom. Kandy was in there, sitting on the built-in window seat. When she heard me coming in, she glanced over her shoulder, then rolled her eyes. She was feistier, now that she was pregnant, and a lot more emotional. She would cry at the drop of a hat, and get angry just as quick. It was strange, but as I was told, hormones are powerful. A pregnant Kandy wasn't to be taken lightly.

"Cake?" I offered, holding a plate out to her.

She narrowed her eyes as she looked at it then turned away. "I'm not hungry."

I exhaled, placing the plates on top of the dresser and then walking to her. Sitting beside her on the bench, I looked her over. She was wearing yoga pants and a Nike shirt. *Did she really think she was going to walk in those stupid fucking slippers on a treadmill, though?*

"Look, I know you think I'm being a—"

"An overbearing jackass?" she snipped, cutting me off. "Yeah, you are." She folded her arms.

"I'm just trying to protect you and the baby, Kandy. Okay? I feel like you aren't taking this as seriously as you should be."

"How, Cane? I'm not just going to sit around and get fat. I need to move—do something! I've binge-watched literally everything on Netflix and all of the On Demand movies. I need to move—to do something."

"You're in school now," I noted.

"Yeah, but you have Lora drop me off every day, just to make sure I get there safely." She rolled her eyes.

"You only have one more month before we find out if you're okay to carry this baby or not, Kandy. We haven't had any mishaps happen yet, thank God, but I don't want you taking this for granted. Maybe nothing has happened because you've been here, and you've been careful."

She didn't respond, just lowered her head.

"Are you having regrets?"

She avoided my eyes.

"Kandy?"

"I don't know, Cane," she muttered.

"I know we didn't plan for this. I get that. You weren't expecting it, and sometimes the surprises look like they are setting us back, but it's only temporary, baby. I promise." A tear slid down her cheek, and I sighed, wrapping a hand around her head and bringing it to my chest. "Don't cry, Kandy. Listen to me, okay? You've gotten through so much. You'll get through this too."

"I'm just so tired, Cane!" She sobbed into my chest. "My boobs hurt, and my throat is raw every morning. I can't keep a meal down to save my life, but I'm still gaining weight! I feel like I'm in someone else's body!"

"It'll pass, baby. I promise."

"What if all of this is for nothing?" she whimpered. "What if I don't even end up having the baby?"

"You can't think like that, all right? I told you—we're going to think positively."

"I'm trying, but it's hard."

"I know, but you've got this, Kandy. You've done great. It's been eight weeks now, and didn't you tell me that your previous doctor said by the eight-week mark, you'd hear the heartbeat?"

Her cries came to a rapid halt after I said that. She then picked her head up, looking me in the eyes. "Oh my gosh," she breathed. "I get to hear the heartbeat this week."

I smiled. "Did you forget?"

Her throat bobbed as she swallowed. "This Wednesday, right?"

"Yeah, babe. And I'll be right there with you, listening."

"You think we'll hear something?"

"I'm staying positive about it, so yes, I think we'll hear something."

She grinned then, but tried to bite it back. I grabbed her chin, holding it between my forefinger and thumb. "I think once you hear him or her in there, it'll push you in the right direction, make you realize all of this isn't for nothing. Right now, there's a big question in the air for both of us. Hopefully hearing it for ourselves will put us on the right track again."

She nodded, mashing her lips together for a moment.

"I'm sorry," she mumbled, voice feeble. "I don't like arguing with you. I just get so frustrated now—like I literally can't control my feelings."

"Pregnancy woes," I teased, and a laugh bubbled out of her. "Come here." I opened my arms, and she had no problem sliding into them. She curled up on my lap, and I closed my arms, groaning as I held onto her. "Everything will be okay, baby." I kissed her head. "Just stay strong. I know you can."

She nodded, and that was all I needed.

My Kandy wasn't weak. The Kandy I knew had won every battle she'd gone through. She fought for what she wanted, and I knew she really wanted this baby, no matter how tired she was or how much her body was changing.

Her eyes lit up when she realized she'd hear the heartbeat. That was proof enough that she cared, but her fears were popping up, trying to blow those moments of happiness away.

But that's what I was here for. I refused to let anything happen to her or my baby.

We were going to get through this. After all we'd been through, we had no choice.

CHAPTER 12

KANDY

I FELT awful that Cane and I were butting heads so much. We were like two rams in an open field sometimes, going head-to-head over the most trivial things. I couldn't stand it. It wasn't like us, and I knew most of it was my fault, but sometimes I couldn't help the way I felt. I couldn't blame it all on being pregnant, either.

To be honest, I was happy that I could carry a child. I was happy that everything looked okay…but I was terrified of how much my and Cane's life would change. Especially mine. I would no longer have any privacy or moments to myself. I'd lose sleep, which I hated the idea of, because I loved my sleep. It was precious to me, and I cherished it so much. Not only that, but I still hadn't told my dad, and I knew the longer I waited, the angrier he would get about it.

I'd been reading a lot of forums to find advice on embracing the whole pregnancy thing, because it was harder than I thought it would be. I couldn't believe Mom suffered like this, just to have me.

On the flip side, Wednesday had finally arrived.

Cane took me to Dr. Maxine's office, where I was told to do my usual routine with checking in, peeing in a cup, and so on. Dr. Maxine was a lovely woman. She had skin that reminded me of cocoa, a short buzz cut, and a beautiful French accent that I was so envious of. I'd always wanted an accent.

"Okay, Kandy! You ready to hear that little one?" she asked with a bold, white smile.

"Yes!" I grinned at her before looking at Cane. He was standing at my side, watching every little thing she did with soft features. He looked so childlike. He'd never seen any of this happen, so he was intrigued and more than a little excited. It was all we could talk about on the car ride here.

Dr. Maxine asked me to pull my shirt up and to lower my pants just a bit, and then she applied some warm gel. She got straight to it with her ultrasound wand, running it over my lower abdominal area. "Let's see. Where are you, little one?" she whispered softly. She kept moving the wand, narrowing her eyes here and there.

I glanced at Cane nervously. Why couldn't she find the baby? I knew he or she was still there. I could feel it. My heart felt heavy in my chest as she moved to the left, and then she said, "Ah! There is the little bean!"

Relief struck me. *Oh, thank God.*

She kept the wand in place. "Okay, now let me turn on the sound." She pressed a button on the keyboard of the computer beside her, and as soon as she did, a soft thumping sound filled the room. She moved the wand a bit more, and the thumping got even louder.

Thu-thump. Thu-thump. Thu-thump. Thu-thump.

The heartbeat was so quick, like the baby was running his or her own marathon in there.

"Holy shit. Is that the baby's heartbeat?" Cane's voice was winded.

"Yes, it is," she said, smiling at him. "And it sounds so strong and healthy, doesn't it?"

"It does," I cooed. "Oh my gosh, it does!" My eyes welled with tears as I looked at the screen. So there really was someone in there. That little someone was alive, with a beating heart, and I had to protect him or her with everything I had in me.

Cane looked down at me and then leaned forward, cupping the back of my head and kissing my forehead. "You hear that?" His voice was so sweet. So full of joy. "That's *our* baby, Kandy."

"Our baby." I grabbed his hand and kissed the back of it.

"Things are looking as great as ever, too," Dr. Maxine went on. Cane leaned back a bit. "I'm happy with what I'm seeing. Have you been keeping your movements to a minimum for now, like I requested?"

"I have," I said, and Cane cleared his throat, like he was calling bullshit. I gave him a small glare.

"Good. I'd like you to keep it that way, just for the next month or so." She placed the wand down and then grabbed a warm towel from a drawer under the bed to wipe some of the gel off. "The baby seems to be doing well. Considering that you have gone through a loss before, I do think a calm life is a necessity for the duration of your pregnancy. No major traveling or clubbing—things of that nature. Being in a comfortable, stable environment is best. You mentioned you are in school, correct?"

"Yes, but I only have two or three classes a day. I'm careful," I assured her.

"Good. If there is ever a day when you aren't feeling too well, just let me know, and I'll write up a doctor's note for you."

"Okay." She helped me sit up as she stood. "Thank you."

"Do you think she'll be able to carry the baby for the whole nine months?" Cane asked, sounding like my mom.

"Well, with the damage that was done to her uterus before, I wouldn't suggest carrying the baby for the full forty weeks. Instead, what we'd probably do is induce the pregnancy around the thirty-sixth or thirty-seventh week, to be on the safe side, and to avoid ruptures. But I will say that she looks to be on the right track. The baby is growing well."

Cane sighed, clearly relieved. "That's good to know. Thank you."

"Any other questions for me?" Dr. Maxine asked while washing her hands.

We both shook our heads.

"Okay, then. I will see you guys again in two weeks! Feel free to check out with Stacey up front."

We thanked her and left, but not without big grins on our faces. Cane walked with me down the hall that led to the lobby, draping his arm over my shoulders. "See what staying positive does?"

I laughed. "Okay, okay. I know."

He pulled back and grabbed my hand, leading the way to the desk. "How does it make you feel? Hearing the heartbeat?" he asked.

There was only one word that could describe the way I felt in that moment. "Happy," I told him.

But of course, happiness never seems to last long in my world.

∼

THE FOLLOWING DAY WAS PEACEFUL. I read a new book and helped Miss Cane bake an apple pie, but then Friday arrived. Cane got home and seemed a little on edge when he came into the room. I'd just gotten out the shower and was still wrapped in a sky-blue towel.

"What's wrong?" I asked as he paced his way to the closet. He always did that pacing thing when he was bothered.

"We have to have dinner with Eden tomorrow night," he grumbled.

"What?" I walked into the closet as he snatched off his tie. "Why?"

"She came to the Tempt store today. She approved the banner, but informed me that Mr. Miller wants us to have dinner at his house to celebrate the deal. I know she's the one who thought of it. She's trying to fuck with me."

I frowned a little, keeping my annoyance at bay. God, that woman really had no chill. "Then we'll go," I said as he tugged a shirt over his head.

"I don't want to be anywhere near her, to be completely honest."

"But in order for you to stay on good terms with a man who is giving you the opportunity to open many new jobs, you have to go. You can't refuse his hospitality like that, Cane."

"You know what? The shit that annoys me so much is that she specifically asked that I bring you with me. Not me alone, but both of us. She's a shady bitch, and I don't like that shit. She'll try to get between us, make you feel insecure. I can feel it."

I pressed my lips together. I couldn't lie; I did feel a little insecure being in the same room as her. She was beautiful and looked like she could have any man she wanted, but she was fucking with mine. Ugh.

"She won't get between us," I said, walking up to him. "We're stronger than some random ex who thinks she can walk in and twist shit up. She doesn't know our story or what we've been through." I smirked. "Let's have some fun with it. Show her how unbreakable we really are."

Cane smirked at that. "Mmm," he murmured. "I like this new attitude of yours, little one. If I hadn't been ordered to keep my cock away from you, I'd be buried so deep inside you right now." He caught my chin between his fingers as I blushed. "You think you'll be okay going there tomorrow? It'll be the last thing you do for a while. I really don't want you leaving the house much, but since you'll be with me, it should be fine."

"I'll be fine, *man*."

"All right." He dropped a kiss on my lips and pulled his hand away. "Let's do it then, *girl*."

CHAPTER 13

Kandy

To be completely honest, I was nervous as hell, and it didn't help that I was feeling queasy and exhausted. I was standing in front of the floor-to-ceiling mirror in our bedroom, studying myself in a peach, knee-length dress. It was perfect for fall, with sleeves and all. I paired it with wedges, but I couldn't ignore the small bulge at my mid-section. It wasn't the baby yet—probably more bloat than anything.

"God, I look so gross!" I groaned.

"Cut it out!" Cane yelled from the bathroom. "You do not look gross. You look beautiful." He came out of the bathroom, his hair gelled back. He wore black dress pants with a long-sleeved gray button-down. He looked good, and what else was he going to tell his hormone-crazy fiancée? That I was fat?

"I can't even suck in anymore. I'm so bloated. My stomach just sits there." I poked my pudge, and he chuckled, moving closer.

Grabbing my hand and tipping my chin with the other, he

said, "Stop it. You are the most beautiful woman on this planet. Even sexier now that you're carrying *my* baby."

I couldn't fight my smile.

"Where are you guys going?" I looked at the door, and Lora was standing between the frames, looking us over.

"Having dinner with a sponsor." Cane released me to face his sister.

"Oh! Think they'll mind if I tag along? I'm starving!"

"It's bad manners to bring more mouths to feed, Lora," Cane stated.

"The guy's rich, right? I'm sure he doesn't mind feeding another person!"

He sighed. He knew he wasn't going to win this fight.

"I'm going! Mom's not cooking tonight because she has a date with Andy. I need food in my belly, so wait for me!"

"Wait, wait, wait," Cane called just before Lora could take off. "A date?"

"Yes, a date." She smirked. "Andy is kinda cute, too."

"She didn't tell me anything about it," he muttered.

"Don't take it personally. I forced it out of her."

"What?" I laughed. "How?"

"I grabbed her phone when she wasn't looking, asked her what all the smiles and giggles were for. I also saw her with a shopping bag and checked it. It was a dress. Scandalous, showed a lot of leg."

"Jesus," Cane groaned, rubbing his forehead.

"What? She can't hide shit from me, okay? I know her like the back of my hand. Anyway, wait for me! I'll meet you downstairs."

She trotted off, and I looked up at Cane as he glanced at me.

"Your sister is a hot mess. Hope you realize that."

He let out a belly deep chuckle. "Trust me, I've known it for years." He picked up his cufflinks from the dresser. "Not sure what my life would be like without her, though. We're eight years apart, and I thought I was fine as an only child, but when she came along, it was easy to forget what it had been like before. Siblings are annoying, but they make life much more interesting."

"I bet." All this sibling talk reminded me of Frankie. I'd texted her a few times over the weeks, and she said she was going to come visit over the summer but never got around to it. I didn't fault her for it, though. I knew she was busy with working, her mom, and Clay.

Deep down, I hoped she'd ended that situation with him. Frankie didn't need that complication in her life, and at the end of the day, she knew it wouldn't have been right for them. But, life is life, I supposed. Shit happened, and I couldn't blame her for how she felt. Sometimes love and lust chooses you, not the other way around. I, of all people, knew exactly what that was like.

～

WE TOOK Cane's Aston Martin to Mr. Miller's mansion in Concord. His home was probably three times bigger than Cane's, with green grass and freshly trimmed hedges and *so* many lights on the lawn. I was kind of glad Cane was a minimalist. This mansion looked complicated. I was certain that if I lived there, I would get lost.

Cane parked in the large driveway behind two silver SUVs. My heart clanged against my rib cage as we walked to the door. I had my hand in Cane's, and Lora was following behind us.

Cane rang the doorbell, and when it opened, we were greeted by an older man. I would have assumed he was Mr. Miller, but the black and white tux and white gloves gave him away. He let us inside and said, "Good evening, Mr. Cane. Miss Jennings. And..." The man looked puzzled as he spotted Lora.

"Lora Cane," she filled in as she walked past him with a big smile on her face. "Don't worry, I'm just the tagalong. No formalities for me."

"Very well, Miss Lora Cane. I'm Brandon, and I will be taking care of you all this evening. Also, I don't think Mr. Miller will mind that you have joined us. There is plenty of wine to go around, plus he loves having company." He extended his arms, putting his attention on me. "Can I take your jacket?"

"Oh—yeah, sure." I shrugged out of my leather jacket and handed it to him. He folded it over his arm and then turned to Lora, but she was already shrugging her way out of her jean jacket. She dumped it on his arm and continued her smile.

"Thanks," she breathed. "Where is this wine you were speaking of?"

Brandon turned to hang the jackets on the coat rack in the corner. "Right this way." He led the way down a wide-open corridor. The floors were made of dark hardwood, the ceiling so high you could jump on a trampoline in this place. There were brown beams in the ceiling and paintings on the walls, all of them splashed with colors and made up of random things like houses, planes, and boats. No family pictures, though.

"Lora," Cane hissed as she met at his side. "Have some class, will you? You already aren't supposed to be here."

"Class?" Lora laughed. "What the hell is that?"

"I'm not kidding," he mumbled.

"Neither am I. Never heard of it."

I couldn't help laughing.

"Don't encourage her," Cane said in my ear.

I pressed my lips, but my smile couldn't be contained. We finally made it to a foyer. A black piano was in the corner, right in front of a large bay window. There was a man at the keyboard playing a sweet, welcoming melody.

"Wow...this man went all out for this dinner, didn't he?" Lora looked all around.

"I'm sure he isn't the one who set this up," Cane said, slightly agitated.

"What do you mean?"

"Cane!" A voice chimed to our right, and we all looked to

find it. Of course it was Eden. And of course she looked very pretty. She wore a halter-top black dress that hugged every curve her body. Her hair was dark, straight, and sleek, and her makeup looked like it'd been done professionally. If she'd hired a butler and a pianist, I'm sure she'd hired a makeup artist too. She strutted toward us in her high heels, focused solely on Cane.

Cane stood where he was.

"I'm so glad you made it!" She was still chipper, still ignoring her other guests.

"Eden, you remember my fiancée Kandy." Cane draped an arm around my shoulder.

"Of course how could I forget her fresh, youthful face?" Her smile was forced as she met my eyes and then extended her arm, offering a hand. "I didn't get to formally introduce myself."

"That's okay," I said evenly. "No formalities for me."

Lora cracked up at that one. "Oh, boy."

Eden looked from me to Lora, narrowing her eyes. "I'm sorry…who are you?"

"Oh, I'm Cane's sister. I was informed the guy who owned this place was rich, and I didn't know what I wanted for dinner, so I just tagged along. I'm certain there will be plenty of food." Brandon walked around Eden with a tray of wine glasses, offering one to Lora. *Saved by the butler.*

"Thank you, Brandon," Lora said.

Brandon offered one to Cane, me, and Eden, but Eden didn't take one. I grabbed mine, but didn't sip.

"Well, anyway," Eden sighed. "Dinner will be right this way." She turned and walked back down the hallway she came from. We followed after her, Cane's hand dropping to grab mine. Eden's walk had far more hip swaying than necessary—just another desperate attempt to grab attention.

"Damn, that bitch is desperate," Lora snickered over her glass of wine. I grinned. I was glad Lora came. She lightened the mood, and had no filter whatsoever. I also could tell she'd already gotten under Eden's skin.

Eden rounded a corner, and we were met with a large dining table surrounded by six seats and topped with fresh, steaming food of all sorts. A man was standing in the corner with a cellphone pressed to his ear. He had brown skin and dark brown eyes, his head bald and a graying beard. He looked to be in his sixties.

"Dad, your guests are here." Eden met up to him, and the man looked over his shoulder. He wrapped up his call and then turned to look at us with a warm smile.

"Mr. Cane!" he bellowed, raising his hands in the air. "I am so honored to have you here!"

"The pleasure is mine, Mr. Miller." Cane released me to shake his hand.

"And I see you brought two lovely women with you," he noted, looking between me and Lora. "Which one is the fiancée?"

"She is." Cane gestured for me to come closer with a cock of his head. "Kandy, this is Gerald Miller. Gerald, Kandy." Cane looked at Lora, who was sipping her wine. "That wild thing over there is my sister," he teased.

"Whatever, dude." Lora lowered her glass and shook Mr. Miller's hand after he'd gripped mine.

"Well, I'm happy to have you all here. I'm sorry Mrs. Miller can't join us tonight. She's in Dallas, visiting her sister, but on the other hand, the food was just finished by my chef, who makes terrific soul food. Come on"—he lifted a hand toward the table —"Sit. Let's eat."

∽

FOR THE MOST PART, dinner wasn't too bad. Mr. Miller was a nice guy, but I did notice Eden trying to give Cane seductive eyes. She would cut her eyes at me, here and there, when she thought no one else would notice.

"Kandy?" Eden called. "Something wrong with the food?"

I looked up. "Oh, no. Not at all. I'm just not very hungry right now."

"Really? Who comes to a planned dinner without an appetite?" Her smile was faux.

"Actually, she has a very good reason for not eating," Lora cut in, finishing whatever bite of food she'd taken.

"Oh yeah?" Eden lowered her fork. "And what reason might that be?"

"What? Can't you tell?" Lora laughed.

"Lora, not now," Cane hissed.

"Tell what?" There was annoyance in Eden's voice. She really didn't like Lora. It was comical, really.

"She has a glow to her, you know? And they mostly say that about women who are expecting or getting laid really good." Lora picked up her wine glass and sipped, like she hadn't just dropped a bomb on the table.

"Lora!" I gasped.

"Oh, wow? Are you really?" Mr. Miller asked, his eyes lighting up as he looked me over. I forced a smile, wanting so badly to cut my eyes at Lora. She'd had one too many and her I Don't Give A Fuck attitude was showing more and more.

Cane pressed his lips and nodded at Mr. Miller when he swung his eyes over to him. I could tell he didn't want to talk about it right now, but also didn't want to be rude by changing the subject. "Yes, we are."

"Oh, man! Congratulations! I tell you, having a kid...there's nothing like it. They bring a lot of joy to your world." Mr. Miller reached over to rub Eden's shoulder. "If it weren't for Eden, my country club would be a sitting duck."

Eden forced a smile at him before looking between Cane and

me. "A baby, huh?" She sat back in her chair and took a few hard gulps of wine. "No wonder you haven't touched your wine."

I smiled, like, *really* smiled at her.

"I almost forget what it's like having a baby," Mr. Miller went on, like he was in a daze. "It's been so long. You know, I keep telling Eden to get a husband, get married, live a good, happy life, but she's a workaholic like her father, I suppose." Mr. Miller went on and on, and Cane nodded and chatted with him, but I couldn't help passing glances at Eden.

During the rest of dinner and even through dessert, I noticed Eden was no longer looking at Cane so much, but at me. Lora was having a field day with all of the food, especially enjoying the six-layer chocolate cake for dessert.

Now, I wasn't a big fan of doing petty things, but when it came to women who thought they were better for Cane than I was just because they were older, I wasn't above throwing a little shade. So whenever Cane looked at me and asked if I was okay, I'd say, "Yeah, babe. I'm okay," loud enough for everyone at the table to hear me clearly. And when he grabbed my hand and kissed my knuckles like he always did, I blushed and giggled. Okay—the blushing thing I always did, but the giggling was to amp the dramatics.

When it was time to go, I almost skipped out the door. Mr. Miller said goodnight to all of us at the front door, and Eden did the same, though this time she decided to hug us. She hugged Cane first, of course, but it was a small hug. A simple one. No full body contact or her groin meshing into his. A friendly hug, which confused me. She started to hug Lora, but Lora held up a hand.

"Shakes only, lady love." Lora extended her arm, and Eden was perplexed, but took Lora's hand anyway, giving it a shake.

And then Eden was facing me. She let out a long sigh, looking me all over. "What a lucky girl you are," she sighed. "Especially to have such a great, handsome man." Her eyes shifted over to Cane's, who'd narrowed his in exchange. She then looked over her shoulder at Mr. Miller, who was talking to Lora about something pertaining to his country club. "One thing Cane probably didn't tell you about me is that I grew up with a single mother. It was hard watching her sometimes. My father had an affair with my mother, and having me changed everything for her. Luckily, I'm not the kind of woman who would feel proud about coming between a child and his or her parents. I watched it all my life with my mother, and it was the worst feeling in the world. Maybe that's why I am the way I am." Her smile was small. "Have a great night, *Mrs. Cane.*"

I gave her a nod while Cane tugged on my hand.

"Have a good night, Eden." Cane lead the way to his car, Lora trailing behind us.

"I'm so confused," I said when we got inside and the doors were closed. "What in the hell was that?"

"That, I assume, was her way of saying she would back off." Cane and I looked ahead at Eden, who was walking back inside with her father at her side. I could tell Mr. Miller really did love her. He was proud of Eden—probably proud to be able to call a child his own, period.

"Huh."

"Bitches get weak when babies are involved," Lora slurred, and I laughed. She'd clearly had one too many glasses of wine. "I can't wait to see what your baby will look like, Kandy." Lora leaned between the console, and Cane chuckled, glancing over as Lora twirled a loose piece of my hair. "You have such great skin and nice cheekbones, and Cane has those weird eyes that always seem to change colors with the seasons or his emotions. That baby is going to turn all of us to mush."

I couldn't fight my grin. I was glad she was speaking the baby into existence, and not treating it like a maybe or a hopeless feat. I needed to do the same, because this baby was going to happen. I was going to have him or her, and I was going to love the baby with my whole heart.

Lora finally sat back and rested her head on the window, watching the streetlights, and Cane grabbed my hand, bringing it on top of the middle console and squeezing it.

He didn't have to say much in this moment. His full smile said it all—he couldn't wait to see our baby too.

CHAPTER 14

Kandy

The entire house knew that between two and four in the evening, I took my daily nap. No ifs, ands, or buts about it. By that time of day, I was completely exhausted, and nothing could keep me up. But for some reason, my man wanted to disturb my peaceful slumber, and I wasn't happy with it.

"Kandy," Cane called.

"Ugh, Cane." I groaned, pushing his hand away when he tapped me again.

"Kandy, wake up."

"What?"

I rolled onto my back, looking through the corner of my eye at him. "I need to show you something," he said.

"Can it wait? I'm really tired today."

"No. It can't. And you're tired every day. Plus, Lora said you've been sleeping since two, and it's now six. You gotta get up." He grabbed my hand and tugged on it. "Come on, *girl.* I ain't got all day."

I huffed a laugh, throwing an arm over my face. "You're insane, *man.*"

He chuckled, bending over to kiss my exposed lips. Then his lips trailed down to my neck. "Up, baby. I think you'll love what I have to show you."

Sighing, I caved and sat up, rubbing my eyes. He helped me out of bed, and I felt the weight drop right to my lower belly, making me lurch. "It better be worth it, Cane. I mean it."

"Ohh, you are a grumpy little thing," he teased with a grin.

I rolled my eyes, but I couldn't *not* smile. With my hand still in his, Cane led the way downstairs and through the foyer. We walked down the hallway to the kitchen, where the lights were off. Cane flipped the switch on, and out of nowhere there was a loud "SURPRISE!"

I gasped with a hand to my chest as Mom, Dad, Miss Cane, Lora, and Frankie stood in a kitchen full of colorful balloons. "Oh my gosh!" I squealed, staring up at Cane. "What is this?"

"Just a little something for my queen." He shrugged. "Happy birthday, little one." Cane kissed my cheek while I looked ahead at the two-tier cake and food on the counters, then at Mom and Dad. I focused most on Dad and said a quick prayer of gratitude that I wasn't showing yet, or he would have had a fit.

"Happy Birthday, kid," Dad said, meeting up to me and hugging me tight. I hugged him back.

"I'm surprised you guys are here. My birthday isn't for two more days."

"Well, Cane planned something a bit earlier," Mom said. "And I'm glad he did."

"Oh—I got you something." Dad reached for a wrapped gift on the counter behind him and handed it to me.

"What is it?"

"Open it and see."

I tore the gift wrap off and noticed it was a jewelry box. I looked up at Dad warily before opening it. It was a pair of diamond earrings, this set bigger than the pair he'd given me when I was seventeen.

"Oh my gosh!"

"You like them?" he asked, his smile getting bigger.

"Dad, are you kidding? I love them!"

"Your mother helped me pick them out. Consider it a gift from both of us."

"I love it so much. Thanks you guys." I hugged them both around the neck.

"Okay, okay! Enough of the sappy mess! I need to say hello to my bestie!" Frankie grabbed my arm and twisted me around. She pulled me in a for a hug, and I laughed, as did my parents, then squeezed her just as tight as she squeezed me. "So…I didn't bring a gift, but I do want to plan a night out with you tonight. I'm off—no work. Clay is taking care of Mom."

"A night out?" Cane asked, stepping up beside us.

"Yes, Mr. Cane. A night out. She may not be free, but she's still young and wild, right, K.J.?"

I laughed nervously. Poor Frankie. I still hadn't told her about the baby—not that I didn't want to. I just didn't want to tell too many people when things could end up awry. Every person I tell is someone I have to un-tell if things go wrong, and I can't imagine how hard that would be for me.

"Guys, how about we try some of the appetizers Miss Cane made?" Mom suggested, but she made a face that said *"go tell your best friend why you can't and shouldn't go out."*

"Please, eat as much as you'd like," Miss Cane urged. "I think I may have made too much food," she laughed.

"No such thing, Mom," Lora said. "Whatever is left over, I'm sure I'll pig out on it once I light up a joint."

Miss Cane shooed her playfully and started serving food to everyone.

"Frankie, I need to talk to you." I grabbed her hand and led her out of the kitchen. On my way out, I peered back at Cane, who nodded at me.

When we were in the den and out of earshot, Frankie asked, "What is it? What's going on?"

"Um...I don't think I should go out tonight."

She frowned a bit. "Why not? I haven't seen you in forever!"

"Yeah, I know but...I just found out something, and it means I have to take it easy for a while."

"Something like what? Are you sick?"

"No...it's just that...I'm pregnant," I said, as more of a question than a statement, and Frankie's eyes nearly bulged out of her head.

"Holy shit!" she gasped. "What? But I thought you couldn't have—"

"We all thought so, but I am. I've been sick, and so tired, but I go to the doctor often, and the baby is still there. I keep thinking I'll wake up one day, and it'll all be a dream, but it's not. It's really, really happening."

"Shit, K! That is so amazing!" Frankie wrapped me up in her arms again, and I laughed over her shoulder. "Why the hell didn't you tell me sooner?" She pulled back, gripping my shoulders and looking at me with an even deeper frown than before.

"I didn't want to jinx myself by telling the whole world, you know? Plus I'm still really high risk. There's a chance things could go wrong."

"And you didn't think to tell me?" a deep voice interjected, and I gasped, looking to my right. Dad was walking around the corner with a grimace.

"Dad, I—"

"You're pregnant, Kandy? Is that what I just heard?"

Frankie took a step back as Dad got closer. I stayed in place, and a defeated sigh pushed through my lips as I said, "Yes, Dad. I'm pregnant."

"What the hell?" he barked, and footsteps sounded right after. Cane was down the hallway, standing behind Dad. "What the hell is going on?" he demanded.

"You got her pregnant *again*?" Dad snapped, swinging around and pointing a finger in Cane's face.

"Derek!" Mom popped up around the corner, grabbing Dad's arm. "Stop it!"

"Did you know?" Dad shouted in Mom's face.

"Yes, I knew," she snapped, voice firm.

"And you didn't tell me? What kind of wife keeps a secret like that from her own husband?"

"The kind of wife who knows her husband would throw a damn tantrum over the news!" she retorted.

"It's not her fault, Dad!" I yelled. "I told her not to tell you. I wanted to tell you myself when the time was right."

"Oh yeah? When? When the baby is born?"

"I was going to tell you," I assured him. "I—I was just trying to make sure everything was really going to happen. I knew you wouldn't react well to it."

"Damn right I'm not going to react well to it!" Dad shook his head and scoffed, looking between me and Cane. "You're both reckless and stupid, and if she suffers another loss because you couldn't keep your dick—"

"DEREK!" Mom hollered. "Outside. *Now!*" She pointed at the door, and Dad glared hard at Cane before putting his focus on her. I'd never seen Mom get so angry with Dad, ever—especially not when it came to defending me.

When Dad realized how dead serious she was, he grunted and turned away, rushing past Lora and Miss Cane, who were standing in the hallway, and out the door. Mom went after him and the door slammed closed.

The whole house was quiet. To say I was embarrassed was an understatement.

I lowered my head, squeezing my eyes shut. "He always does this. Lets his temper get the best of him. He's a fucking asshole."

"He's upset, Kandy. You knew he'd react this way," Cane murmured.

"I don't care. He needs to grow the hell up already."

Cane sighed, wrapping his arms around me and kissing the top of my head.

"Lora, Mom, take Frankie to the kitchen with you. Make her some food."

"Sure. Yeah," Lora breathed.

"For the record," Frankie said, rubbing my arm. "I'm super fucking happy for you guys. You'll make great parents."

Her words made me smile. Just a little. "Thanks, Frank."

When she was out of the room, it was just Cane and me. "I'm sorry he said that to you," I whispered. "I should have told him before now and spared all of this drama and embarrassment."

"Don't worry about it. I understand his frustration."

"But it doesn't make it right, and it doesn't mean he can say whatever he wants to say to you just because he's upset with you. He doesn't have to be a dick about everything. You're my fiancé, I love you, and he should respect that."

"Well, first of all, you haven't told him we're getting married, so he has no idea we're engaged. Second of all, this is a hard pill for your dad to swallow, Kandy. He has to get used to the idea of us. Men aren't like women. It's harder for us to process and accept certain things. We were friends once. Now we're just…*here*. Stuck in an awkward situation, trying to live through it."

"Well he has to learn to accept it and let things go. Not just for my sake anymore, but the baby's too. I want the baby to have a good, happy grandpa. Not one who will talk shit about his or her dad because he isn't on good terms with him."

"Derek isn't like that. He won't spew hatred to an innocent child, especially his own grandkid."

Ugh. For his sake, I hoped he was right.

The front door opened, and Mom came back inside. "Let him cool off," she said, then forced a smile at us before closing the door and walking down the hallway to get to the kitchen.

"You heard her. Come on," Cane said. "We aren't going to let that ruin your birthday."

"It's already ruined," I muttered as he draped an arm over my shoulders and escorted me back to the kitchen. Lora had music playing on her portable speaker, a song by Dua Lipa, and I was glad she, Frankie, and Miss Cane were focusing on the actual party and not what had just happened several minutes ago.

I suppose we were all used to the chaos because we all dealt with some form of it. None of us had lived a stable life. It was easy to brush off the minor things, like arguments and fights. And with that in mind, I decided to go along with it. Yes, Dad was upset, but he would cool down and get over it. His temper always got the best of him in the heat of the moment, but once it was over, he'd return to settle it.

And sure enough, after we all ate a slice of cake and recited lyrics to our favorite songs, Dad was back. He stood at the mouth of the kitchen, looking at all of us.

"Calm now?" Mom asked, quirking a brow at him.

He merely ignored her. "Kandy...can we talk?" he asked, and I placed my plate down. I glanced at Cane, who gave me a slow blink and a nod, and then walked past Dad, rounding the corner to get to the backyard. I sat on one of the lounge chairs as Dad closed the door behind him. He met up beside me, taking the lounge chair next to mine.

We were quiet for several seconds. From where we were, I could still hear the music playing in the kitchen, as well as some laughter.

"Look, I'm sorry for my temper before," he finally said. "I just... I don't understand. Why didn't you just tell me? Why did I have to be last to know?"

"Because I didn't know how to tell you, Dad. And I knew you would blow up like you always do. You're like an Angry Bird."

At that, he shook his head, but he couldn't hide his smirk. "Kandy...the odds of you getting pregnant were slim. Your mom told me all about it. Of course I'd want to know right away that you are."

"I know. I'm sorry." I focused on the ground.

"How many weeks?"

"I just hit the fourteen week mark."

"Hold up...fourteen whole weeks you've been pregnant, and you didn't tell me?" His brows drew together, but his eyes were soft. Playful. "If you still lived with me, I would ground your butt right now, you know that?"

I laughed.

"I'm just...shocked, I guess," he went on. "I didn't see it coming."

"Well...then, I guess you'll be even more shocked to find out that Cane and I are engaged now."

"Engaged?" Dad's eyes got even wider. "Are you kidding me? Anything else you haven't told me?"

"No, Dad. That's it."

He sighed and was quiet for several seconds. "Engaged, huh?" he finally said.

"Yep. He asked me when we were in Belize. I said yes."

"When's the wedding?"

"Next year, after I graduate. Well, hopefully. I'm not sure how things will work with the baby."

"Good. I'm glad you're finishing school first." He looked me over. "You sure you're ready to be a mother and a wife? Being a spouse is hard work, but being a parent is even harder. You see what we had to go through with you, right?"

I pushed him with my elbow, giggling. "I was not that bad."

He shrugged. "You were a nightmare at times, but overall, a pretty good kid."

"I don't know if I'm ready...but if I'm at fourteen weeks, and still carrying this baby...I'm here for it. I was told by my doctor that the first thirteen weeks were my highest risks for miscarriage, but I've made it. The baby is still in there, and if I'm meant to have him or her and become mother, I will make sure I'm ready."

Dad put on a small smile and then lowered his head. "You're a good person, Kandy. You know that? I guess I didn't screw up with you after all." With a grin, he stood and opened his arms, and I pushed out of my chair, walking into his embrace. With a deep exhale, he said, "You've put me through a lot of shit...but I love you more than anything. The baby is...well, I'm not going to lie. It'll be hard for me to wrap my mind around for a while, but I'm here for you. For whatever you need."

"I know, Dad."

"Good." He dropped a kiss on my forehead. "Now let's get back to the party."

Dad walked with his arm slung over my shoulders, back to the house. In the kitchen, Lora and Frankie were taking shots of whiskey—the crazies—and Mom, Cane, and Miss Cane were laughing at Frankie's face every time she took one.

Everyone was smiling. Happy. For the first time ever, we were all together—all the people I loved—and we were enjoying ourselves. We all had our issues, yes, but when the room was full of life like this, nothing outside of it mattered.

These people? They were my family. I had no idea what I would do without any of them, and knowing that my baby would have their love was going to be worth it. Of course, Dad didn't really talk to Cane for the rest of that night. Cane didn't bother making an attempt to speak to him. They kept their distance, and it was fine, just so long as they didn't end up in each other's face all over again.

Around 9:00 p.m., Mom and Dad left. They had to work in the morning and still had the drive back to Atlanta. I hugged them goodbye and watched them go. When I could no longer see their tail lights, I went back to the kitchen.

"Frankie, you should definitely stay the night," Miss Cane insisted as I rounded the corner. "I refuse to let you drive after taking five shots of whiskey."

"Dude, I'm totally fine! I can drive!" Frankie tried convincing her, but by the stern look on Miss Cane's face, I knew it wasn't going to happen.

"She is not fine," Lora tittered. "That bitch is *fucked up*."

"I guess this is my night out, huh?" Frank giggled and threw her arms around my neck.

"Yeah, you're drunk," I laughed. "You're staying the night, and we have a few extra rooms, so no excuses."

"Yep. You can sleep it off," Cane said.

"Okay, okay. Fine. Well, if that's the case…" Frank pulled away from me to pick up her shot glass and the half-empty bottle of whiskey. She topped her glass off and then raised it in the air. "I'll keep sipping on this *whis-kay!* Cheers to you, Cane and Kandy! I hope the baby is just as amazing as you guys are!"

"Fuck yeah!" Lora squealed, picking up the whole bottle of whiskey. Apparently, she was just as drunk as Frankie. "Cheers!"

They clinked glasses, and Cane, myself, and Miss Cane laughed while Lora drank straight from the bottle while Frankie downed her shot.

They were insane, I swear, but I wouldn't have traded them for anyone or anything in this world.

CHAPTER 15

Cane

Having a pregnant fiancée was hard work. There I was, thinking it would be a breeze—a simple nine months of bliss and happiness—it was anything but.

For one, I was stressed. Stressed about the baby. Stressed about Kandy and her comfort and health. I knew she was getting tired of being home so much. She still went to school for her classes, but she'd come right back home, doing as I told her to.

At first, I felt bad for being so insistent about her modified bedrest, but she and I both agreed we would do whatever it took to protect the baby and keep her healthy. When we got deeper into winter, it only intensified my stress. Lora had gotten a cold, so I told her she had to quarantine herself in Mama's bedroom so Kandy wouldn't get sick. Of course Lora was annoyed by it, but I didn't give a damn.

Not only that, but Kandy was starting to show and...I don't know. There was something about the sight of her carrying my baby that had me reeling. When she undressed around me, revealing her prodding belly, all I wanted to do was lie her on the bed and thrust my cock between her legs. I wanted to kiss her from head to toe, but mostly her stomach, where my baby rested. I wanted her to know that I put that baby there. Me.

I couldn't have sex with her for nine months, and if I could be perfectly honest, it was fucking torture already. I had made a mental countdown to the days I'd be able to make her body mine again—once my baby was born, and she'd healed properly.

In the meantime, I settled with kissing her…until one night, she surprised me.

"Lay down," she ordered, walking out of the bathroom in her night gown.

I was sitting on the bed, scrolling through emails on my phone. I'd just gotten back in town from Charleston. Kandy waltzed to the bed, sweeping her eyes all over me. She climbed on top of it, and my brows dipped as I met her gaze.

"What are you doing, Kandy?" I asked, as she tugged on the waistband of my pants. I lifted my hips as she pulled them down to my ankles.

"We haven't been able to do anything in months. My morning sickness is going away and the smells don't drive me crazy as much anymore. I need to please you for putting up with my shit so far."

At that, I laughed. "Please me? And how exactly are you gonna do that?"

"I'm going to give you what you want," she murmured. "What you need."

"And what do I need baby?"

"My mouth…around your *cock*."

A deep groan filled my throat. She didn't even have to touch me for me to get hard. It'd been five and a half months of no play. I'd had the urge to jack off, but a part of me wanted to wait until we could do something again, just so we could experience the anxiousness together, but I doubted I'd make it that long.

"You sure about this?" I asked as her mouth hovered over the tip of my cock.

"Positive," she sighed, and then she parted her rosy lips, sealing her mouth around my tip. She gripped my shaft, and the combination of her soft hand and slick mouth was enough to have me throbbing.

"Shit," I groaned. She took me deeper into her mouth, almost choking on it. "Look up at me," I ordered. "I want you to watch me while you suck my cock."

She moaned around me, the vibrations sending spasms down to my balls. Her hand shifted up and down, fisted around my cock, pumping lightly while her tongue swirled around the head. Not once did she take her eyes off of me. She knew I loved that—when her eyes were on mine while my cock was in her mouth.

A deeper groan built up in my throat as I lifted a hand and pressed it to the back of her head. My fingers got tangled in her hair, and I clutched a lock of it, forcing her face down, making her take down every inch.

She gagged around me and then came back up for air.

"Do that again, baby," I rasped, and she had no problem doing so. She took me all in again, her eyes dropping for just a moment to concentrate—to breathe—and when she came back up, her big brown eyes were on mine again. "Fuck, you look so sexy." She kept doing that same action again, over and over, taking my cock as deep as she could into her mouth while her hand stroked and pumped the base of my cock. "Shit, I'm about to cum."

Like I said, it'd been months, and in this moment, patience was not on my side. Gripping either side of her head, I tilted my hips and shoved my cock down her throat. She made a muffled noise, but stayed in place, and a thunderous groan ripped right through me as my cum spilled down her throat.

"Oh, fuck, baby!" I couldn't even control my voice. That's how intense my orgasm was. I shuddered as she kept slurping and lapping me up, drinking every drop of my cum. With my hands still on her head, I pulled her head up and watched as she kissed the tip of my dick, making it twitch. "Fuck," I panted. "You're still so full of surprises."

She grinned, and I released her. She climbed up beside me, throwing an arm around my waist and resting the side of her face on my cheek. "Whenever you need to let go a little, just tell me. I still want to please you."

"I know you do, but it's fine, Kandy. I will live."

"I like going down on you," she giggled. "I like when you lose control."

"I see that," I chuckled.

She sighed. "Have you thought of names?"

"No, not really." We'd decided at Kandy's 20-week appointment that we didn't want to find out the gender. We figured whether it was a boy or a girl, we would love him or her regardless. Of course, we shopped for unisex colors, like yellows and greens, and Kandy and Lora had even started decorating one of the extra bedrooms, setting it up as the nursery. We were excited for the baby, and even happier that this miracle was happening right in front of our very eyes.

"I think I'll leave the name-picking up to you. I'm not really good with names," I murmured.

"I've been Googling some, searching on Pinterest, but there are so many. What about Leo for a boy?"

"Meh. I know a Leo, and he's an asshole. What else you got?"

"Okay...what about Valerie for a girl?"

"Hmm...I kind of like that. Put it on the list. Any others?"

She sat up, pressing down on the bed with a flat hand. "Okay... this one is going to sound weird...but what about Chance, for a boy?"

"Chance? Like take a *chance*?"

"Yes!" She broke out in a laugh.

"Isn't there a rapper with that name?"

"Yes, but that's not why I want to use that name. The way I see it, this baby is our fighting chance, and if someone ever asked, I'd have no problem explaining how."

I raised a brow. "Wow. Now that you explain it, it makes sense." I looked into her eyes. "I like that."

"So Valerie for a girl, and Chance for a boy?"

He smirked. "I can get down with those."

"Good." She climbed on my lap, and her belly settled between us. I felt a kick in my abdomen and smiled. The baby was moving. My baby. "I love you so much," she said to me, her arms laced around my neck.

"And I love you, little one." I kissed her upper lip. "So much."

I'll be honest, I never thought there would be a day when I was excited to have a baby on the way. My life had been so chaotic and busy that I deemed it impossible, yet on my lap was a pregnant beauty, five and a half months along, and in her womb was my child. *Mine.* I'd planted that seed, and we were watching it grow.

I never knew such happiness existed, but now that it was happening, I never wanted to let go of it.

CHAPTER 16

Cane

3 1/2 Months Later

REMEMBER when I said if there was too much peace in my life, a storm would always come rolling by? Well, I could feel it coming, and for the first time in my life, I knew this was a storm that was going to make me suffer. I'd drown in its treacherous waters with no one to save me. Because sometimes, we couldn't be saved. Sometimes we got swept away with no one to help us.

My phone buzzed on my desk, and I saw it was a text from Kandy. I remembered the day she texted me. March 20th.

> **Kandy: Not feeling well today. Can't tell if I'm having really bad Braxton-Hicks or actual contractions.**

> **Me: Need me to come get you?
> Take you to see Dr. Maxine?**
>
> **Kandy: No. I think I just need to lie down.
> Tired. Text me when you're on the way home.**
>
> **Me: I will. Get some rest.
> If you need anything, ask my mom or Lora.
> They're there to help.**
>
> **Kandy: I will**

I'D TOLD Cora I couldn't fly out of town for three months straight. The work was going to have to come to me since Kandy had just hit the eight and a half month mark and the baby was due at any time. Not only that, but the Braxton-Hicks contractions were getting stronger.

Her doctor suggested that I remain close, and also mentioned that since Kandy was such high risk, that the baby could come way before forty weeks. Her induction was scheduled in two more weeks, so yeah...this was happening, and the whole pregnancy felt like it had flown by. Kandy was currently at thirty-four weeks, her belly growing rapidly. She thought she looked awful, but to me she was a goddess.

While l worked on writing up emails, my phone buzzed on the desk again. A call from Lora.

"Q!" Lora yelled into the phone. I could hear the worry in her voice, so intense it was almost like I could *feel* it. I jerked to my feet.

"Lora? What's going on?" I asked.

"You need to get to the hospital right now! I'm taking Kandy there. She had a few bad cramps this morning and took a nap, but when she woke up, there was blood on the bed. We're on the way now but she's in a lot of pain."

I didn't have to hear her completely before I was charging out of the office. "I'm coming."

Fuck. My heart pumped faster, going into overdrive. I jammed my thumb into the elevator button, impatiently waiting for it to open.

"Is everything okay, sir?" Cora asked behind me. I turned to look at her. Her face was etched with concern.

"Kandy is having some bleeding," I said as the elevator doors open. I marched in. "Clear my schedule until further notice."

"Of course, sir. You got it. I hope everything is okay."

Yeah, I hoped everything was okay too.

I jogged through the lobby to get to the parking deck. When I was in my car, I started it up and zoomed away from my building. I remained as calm as I possibly could, but it was hard. I was hoping this wouldn't happen, and I prayed to the Almighty above that it was just a false alarm and nothing too bad was happening. Something deep down inside me was always telling me that this bliss wouldn't last, that something was going to disturb our peace and shake up our world. I could handle a lot, but losing her or the baby was something I wasn't so sure I would be able to handle.

To my good fortune, there was no traffic, so I got to the hospital in record time. I shut my car off and jogged to the emergency room, scoping the lobby as soon as I was inside.

"Q!" Lora's voice rose and I looked to the left, spotting her rushing my way with Mama trailing behind her.

"Where is she?" I panted. "Is she okay?"

Lora looked defeated, her eyes watering. "I—I don't know."

I walked around her, going to the counter. "They took a girl back there," I huffed, focusing on the woman behind the counter. "Kandy Jennings. I need to be with her."

The woman seemed unfazed by my urgency. I wanted to slap some sense into her for taking my situation so lightly. "I can't let you back unless you are related to the patient or are a spouse."

"She is my fiancée!" I yelled.

"But you aren't married yet," she stated through clenched teeth. "There is nothing you can do until we hear from the doctor. You'll have to wait out here, sir."

"You have to be fucking kidding me!" I snapped. I glared at the woman behind the counter. "I need to be back there with her. She is my fiancée, and she's carrying *my* baby. If something happens to her again, I'll—"

I didn't even have the words in me. Couldn't complete the thought. If something happened to Kandy, I'd lose it. I swear to God I would.

"Sir, I understand your frustrations, but I can't let you back until we have authorization from the patient. Now, I'll let them know you are waiting, and someone will come speak to you when they can. Until then, please try to relax," she said, but her words were meaningless. She didn't know Kandy's situation or the risks. She didn't know what would happen, and she didn't care.

"Cane?" Mama called, and a hand wrapped around my wrist. "Come sit, son. Please."

Fuck that! How was I supposed to sit when my girl and my baby might have been dying back there, alone? I snatched my hand away and trudged away from the counter, going to a corner. Lora and Mama followed after me.

"If something happens to her or the baby..." I paced back and forth, shoving fingers through my hair.

"She'll be oaky, Q," Lora murmured, but even she didn't sound too convinced.

"You don't know that!"

"Cane..." Mama stepped in front of me, stopping me mid-pace. "She will be okay. What is it that you've always told me?" I stared down at her, but it was hard to see through the thick layer of tears. "She's strong," she reminded me. "That girl is strong. Just sit. Wait."

I snatched my eyes away, looking up at the ceiling, then sniffled, dropping my hands to dig in my pocket. "I need to call Derek."

Mama grabbed my elbow, guiding me to a chair. I found Derek's number, and he answered pretty quickly, his voice sharp. "Cane? What's going on?"

"Hey, D. Something happened with Kandy. She had some cramps this morning but started bleeding, so we're at the hospital now."

"What?" he wheezed. "Is she okay?"

I looked toward the double doors, where they most likely took her. "I don't know. They won't let me back since I'm not related, and I guess they aren't in a position to ask her permission."

"Fuck—all right, I'll call Mindy. We'll get there as soon as we can." He paused, and I heard him sigh before continuing. "It's scary as hell when this happens, not only for her, but for you too, I'm sure." He cleared his throat. "Keep me updated."

"Yeah, I will."

He hung up, and I lowered the phone. We all sat in the lobby, waiting for someone to come out and tell us something—*anything*. My pacing continued, my eyes flicking to the double doors every few seconds. It took two endless hours for someone to finally come out and say Kandy's name.

I rushed toward the man in teal scrubs. He had a face mask pushed down to cover his chin, rectangular-framed glasses around his eyes.

"I'm here for Kandy Jennings," I breathed. "I'm her fiancé, Quinton Cane. How is she doing?"

"She's doing okay, but she specifically asked for you."

I glanced back at Mama and Lora. He wasn't speaking too confidently. Something must have been wrong. "Okay. Where is she?"

"Right this way," he said, turning.

"Keep us updated!" Lora called after me.

I nodded, following the man down a few hallways. He reached

a room at the end of one of the halls on the maternity wing and pushed it open. This room was spacious, full of machines and other devices. A hospital bed was in the middle of the room and lying on top of it was Kandy. When she saw me, she gave me a weak smile, and I rushed for her, hugging her, probably a little too tightly.

"Shit, baby, you can't scare me like that!" I panted. "You okay? How's the baby?"

"I'm okay, and the baby is fine," she assured me, my face clasped in her hands.

"Jesus." I closed my eyes, kissing the middle of her forehead. "What happened?"

"The bleeding wasn't from the baby. They think there may have been a slight rupture so they're doing a C-section to prevent anything worse from happening." Her eyes glistened as she peered into my eyes. "We're going to have a baby soon, Cane."

"Seriously?" I looked back and the man was still there, but was talking to another nurse. "Like, now?"

"Yes," she laughed. *"Now."*

"You're serious?" I cupped her face. "Holy shit, you're serious!" I kissed her everywhere—her nose, her mouth, her cheeks, her forehead, anywhere my lips could find.

A throat lightly cleared behind me, and I let go, looking toward the person. Dr. Maxine was there, a relaxed smile on her lips. "Sorry I'm late, but I'm happy to see you both here!" she sang. "Now, who's ready to have a baby?"

CHAPTER 17

KANDY

I NEVER, in a million years, thought that by age twenty-three, I would become a mother, but it was happening, and this was the moment Cane and I had been waiting for. After months of fatigue, aches, long nights and early mornings, it was happening. After living with doubts and fears and worrying over every little thing, the time had come.

I was given an epidural before the procedure, and when it was time, Dr. Maxine was standing over me while I laid on the table. I really wasn't happy that I had to have a C-section. I read the horror stories, but Dr. Maxine mentioned that a C-section was going to be the safest way to go since Kelly's stabbing had ruptured the lining in the first place. She didn't want any internal bleeding or hemorrhaging to happen, so it made sense.

I didn't care as long as my baby came out healthy. Before the procedure, she'd informed me that my bleeding had stopped, which was good. It meant the baby was okay and that I would be too.

The procedure, to my surprise, was over much faster than I had anticipated. With the epidural in place, I didn't feel a thing. One minute I was lying on the table, anxious while clutching Cane's hand, a paper curtain stretched in front of me, and the next, Cane is gasping sharply, watching Dr. Maxine's every move

"Oh! Here we go, here we go!" Dr. Maxine cheered. "There we go!"

And then I heard a sound—a beautiful sound that made my heart flutter.

The cries of a baby.

In that very moment, it was like my world had slowed down. Like the earth had stopped spinning on its axis, halting time, and dedicating this very second to me. Dr. Maxine had the baby in her hands, and the nurses were clearing his or her nose and mouth. I still couldn't see what gender. Cane was right beside them, and as his eyes traveled down, focused on what was between the baby's legs, he looked my way and rushed to my side, yelling, "It's a boy!"

His voice sounded so distant—muted almost. He kissed me repeatedly, telling me I did so good, but I couldn't look away from the baby.

My baby. My crying, beautiful, baby boy, with a head full of hair and a dimpled little butt.

Dr. Maxine came my way with him, a sweet smile on her lips, and as soon as she lowered him to my chest and his cheek pressed to mine, the earth spun again. His cries came into tune, and they surrounded me, and I loved it. My heart burst with joy and a love that I could not describe.

I cooed to him, hummed to him, letting him know that everything was going to be okay, because it was. Everything was okay, and he was here, and our war had been won. There wouldn't be any more pain or sorrow or surprises. He was here, and he was so, so perfect.

He opened his tiny eyes and looked up at me, and I sobbed and laughed at the same time because they were gray—they looked like Cane's. I picked my head up, and Cane was smiling down at him. He lifted his chin to meet my eyes.

"He's so beautiful," I cried.

"He's perfect," Cane said, cupping my cheek. "Just like his mother."

Cane kissed me hard and deep, and then pulled back to kiss the baby on the forehead.

"We normally don't advise that the mother holds baby right after C-section. We prefer you wait until the anesthesia wears off, so in the meantime, we'll let Dad hold him," Dr. Maxine said.

"That's fine," I smiled at her as she handed the baby to Cane.

Dr. Maxine sewed me up, and after a while, Cane let go of the baby so the nurses could dress him properly. When he was dressed, they took us to a recovery room, and while we were there, they handed him to Cane again. Watching him with his son was beautiful. He couldn't stop staring at him. I'd seen him in awe, but never like this. Never while looking so *vulnerable*, so close to crying tears of pure joy. His eyes glistened as he rocked the baby in his arms, whispering all the while.

"You'll never have to worry about a thing, baby boy," he cooed. "I will love you until the end of time, and even beyond that. You'll have the world."

God. *My heart.*

An hour went by, and my body felt less numb. Finally, I was able to hold my baby in my arms, and of course, I cried instantly. He was warm and snuggly and smelled good. He was so innocent, and all I wanted to do was protect him from any and everything. I couldn't believe the joy I was feeling—the warmth and power in my chest. This was what unconditional love felt like, I realized. It was powerful, emotional, and rooted deep within my soul. Nothing could describe it or replace it—this feeling so monumental it swallowed you whole and refused to let go.

All this time, I wondered how my parents had forgiven me for all I'd put them through, and in this moment, I realized why: this kind of love is irreplaceable. This kind of love steals your heart away, but you don't mind it, because the little thief who has it is worth more than the world can give.

There was a knock on the door about thirty minutes later, and a nurse opened it, just as Cane stood up and grabbed Chance, curling him in his arms. Mom and Dad stood in the doorway, both standing with wide eyes, as if they weren't sure where to go first.

"Oh, Kandy!" Mom gasped, rushing across the room. "Are you okay, sweetie?" She held my face in her hands, looking me all over.

"I'm great, Mom. Everything's okay."

"You had me worried sick," Dad said, moving in next to her, messing up my hair with his hand. He leaned forward. "Sure you're okay?"

"I promise," I laughed.

He stood straight again with a sigh. I looked over at Mom, but she was focused on Cane, who was leaning against the window, facing us. He had the baby in his arms, and Mom had a hand over her mouth, like she couldn't believe what she was seeing. My man looked pretty damn hot holding a baby.

Dad wrapped an arm around Mom's side and urged her forward. She hesitated as she went toward Cane, focused on her grandson.

"It's a boy," I told them.

"Oh my goodness," she breathed. "Oh. My. Goodness. Look at him." She finally met up to Cane, looking the baby all over. "Oh, he's so handsome. So perfect." She put her eyes on Cane's. "Do you mind if I hold him?"

"Of course I don't mind," he said, handing the baby over to her gently.

I looked at Dad, who stood his ground beside me while Mom

cooed and sang and cried over the baby. "Dad," I whispered, nudging him with my hand. "Go meet your grandson."

Dad looked down at me, and for once he'd swallowed his pride and did what I told him to do without putting up a fight. Along the way, he locked his eyes on Cane, who stood a little ways off, watching Mom with the baby. When Dad got closer, he swept his eyes up and down the length of his grandson, finally revealing some emotion. A smile spread across his lips. It was subtle, but still a smile. "Wow," he breathed.

"Here." Mom handed the baby to Dad, and at first he looked alarmed, like he wasn't ready for this part of it yet, but Mom left him with no choice. When the baby was in his arms, he cradled him, holding him close to his chest. Dad's eyes lit up instantly, and there might have even been a glistening.

"Look at that. There are always good things," Mom murmured to him. "Always."

"You've always wanted a boy," Cane said, and Dad looked up at him, his eyes wet and red at the rim. "We can't raise him alone, D. He needs family. Support."

"Oh, trust me," Dad murmured, head shaking. "I'll be here." He studied the baby. "I'll be here every step of the way."

A tear fell down my cheek as I watched my parents with the baby. Cane gave me a sweet, comforting smile before coming up to my side. He planted a kiss on the top of my head, rubbing my shoulder.

There was another knock on the door, but this time it was Lora and Miss Cane. Miss Cane had a bouquet of flowers in hand. Lora came up to me, hugging me tight around the neck. "You ever scare me like that again and I'll beat your ass!" she playfully threatened with a laugh. "You're lucky Cane sent me a text saying you were okay."

Miss Cane had placed the flowerd down and walked around the bed to hug me when Lora let go. "I'm so glad you are okay, love. I knew you would be."

"Thank you," I murmured.

They both washed their hands and then walked to where Cane was now standing. Dad was still holding the baby, not even caring that others were waiting to hold him too. "Okay, Dad. Don't be a baby hog," I joked.

"Yeah, dude. Don't. I want to hold my nephew." Lora stepped up to Dad, extending her arms, her fingers practically screaming the word *gimme*.

Dad handed the baby over proudly, and as soon as Lora had him in her arms, she gushed and said, "Oh my gosh! He's so fucking beautiful! I'm going to die from all of this cuteness!"

Everyone broke out in a laugh, even Dad.

"Look, if you're going to be around when he grows up, you can't bring that potty mouth with you," Dad scolded lightly.

"I'll try...but only for him." Lora ran a finger over the baby's chin, then she turned to look at me. "Kandy? What are you going to name him?"

Everyone turned to face me, waiting for a response. Little did they know that while I was laying on the bed, waiting for the bleeding to the stop, I prayed. I prayed so hard that it would stop and that I would meet the person who'd been kicking and punching me from the inside for the past few months. I wanted to meet him and raise him and do everything for him that I could, so much so that the last thing I'd worried about was his name. That said, I did have an idea, but it wasn't set in stone yet.

"We talked about names, but I'm not sure yet," I murmured.

"Well, it's up to you, babe," Cane said. "You did the hard work, you get the honor."

"What about Duncan?" Lora asked.

"Uh, hell no," Cane laughed, head shaking.

Mom and Dad shook their heads too, Mom's nose scrunched a bit.

"Hey, Duncan is classic and cool as hell. You guys are tripping." Lora waved a hand and shrugged.

I couldn't fight my smile.

CHAPTER 18

Kandy

For the first time in years, I was surrounded by nothing but complete and utter joy. There were no attitudes or resentment. No ugly looks were passed, no hate. I couldn't stop thinking about it, as I sat on the hospital bed. Mom kept busting out in cry-laughing spells, and Dad couldn't stop smiling as he cooed and babbled to the baby.

Who would have thought that someone so tiny could bring us all together in this way? I'm certain Dad still had his issues with Cane, but it seemed, for the most part, he was shoving those issues aside for the sake of the baby and me, and that was all I'd ever wanted—for him to see the bigger, grander picture. To know that even though we had our broken moments, we were still a family.

To my surprise, Frankie came to visit that same day. She walked into the room with blue balloons and a gift basket, unloading it all next to the bed and then squeezing me around the neck. I had Cane send her a text from my phone shortly after the baby was delivered, but I never dreamed she'd be able to get here so soon.

"Oh my gosh, K.J.! You're officially a mama!" she shrieked.

"Isn't that weird?" I laughed.

"Where is the little minion?" Frankie released me and turned to where everyone was. Cane had the baby in his arms and was rocking him gently. He was nervous before, probably scared he'd drop him or something, but the way he looked at Chance...gah, it was everything.

"Oh my goodness!" Frankie cupped her mouth, stepping closer to Cane. "Geez, he's, like, the cutest, chunkiest little thing ever. Look at those cheeks!" Frankie went to the sink to wash her hands then walked back to Cane with her hands out. "Can I?"

"Of course." Cane handed the baby to her with ease, and she sighed as soon as he was in her arms.

"Oh! He's so cuddly!"

Cane smiled, eyes on Chance. Everyone else was looking at the baby too as Frankie nuzzled the tip of her nose across his downy head. Cane's eyes shifted up to me while everyone watched the baby. It was brief, but there was a change in his eyes—a light that I'd never seen before. I had been certain Cane was content before, but in this moment, I think there was a feeling inside him that exceeded happiness.

I know that feeling, because I felt it too.

Happiness was too simple a word for how I felt.

I never wanted these feelings to end.

"I think I know what I'm going to name him," I announced when Frankie handed the baby to me.

"Oh, yeah? What?" Mom inquired.

I snuggled him, and after placing a kiss on his forehead, I looked up at Cane, who smiled down at me like he knew what I was going to say. "He was our fighting chance," I said. "I'm going to name him Chance. Chance Cane."

WITHIN THREE DAYS, I was clear to go. Mom and Dad stayed in a hotel in town and were around a lot. When it was time for me to check out, they were both there waiting. They followed behind us in their car to our house.

I was in the back seat with Chance while Cane drove. I swear, I couldn't stop looking at him even if I tried. And what is it with babies and those long pauses they take before drawing their next breath? It freaked me out when Chance did it, and of course he did it often.

When we arrived, Cane carried Chance to the house in his car seat, heading to the front door to unlock it. My parents met up to me, helping me up the sidewalk and into the house. They helped me unpack and watched Chance while I showered and ate and slept because, yeah, I was super happy, but exhausted too.

Laughing and coughing and even moving were pretty painful, due to the C-section, but when I looked at Chance, I realized I would go through hell and back for him. After all, what was a war without a few battle scars?

Although Chance was a great baby who only cried when he had a dirty diaper, was hungry, or sleepy, he had a terrible latch. Breast-feeding was harder than I expected, and it broke my heart when we'd try and try and still he wasn't getting anything. Chance would cry because he wasn't getting the milk he needed, and I would cry because my baby was hungry, and my nipples hurt, and I was tired as hell.

Cane worked from home so he could be close to me and Chance, and he, Lora, and Miss Cane were great about taking him off my hands when I needed to rest or shower, but feeding him was all up to me, and I refused to give up on it. I swore I would do anything for my baby, so I toughed it out and eventually—okay, a month later—I got the hang of it. It was nice having a support system, and my parents visited every weekend for the first few weeks.

Dad was less hostile about our situation, shoving those feelings aside due to his excitement to be around his grandson. He and Cane talked a lot more, though, which was good. It started with updates about Chance, and then minor sports talk if a game was on, and then they talked about work. They began having full conversations, and I was pleased to see it.

Having a baby while in college was hard, but my professors worked with me. During the first six weeks, I'd enrolled in online classes and did the work from home. When I managed to go to class after those six weeks had passed, Lora or Miss Cane would watch Chance for me for a few hours until I returned. They were good with him, but they spoiled him rotten for sure.

My life revolved around Chance now. I went to college, took care of him, and spent time with Cane. It was a simple life—a routine we'd created—and I was living through it. What we had now felt even more real than what we had before. In a way, Chance completed us. He made us happy. He was a beautiful baby, with chunky thighs and small toes and chubby cheeks. His skin was a few shades lighter than mine, and a bit darker than Cane's—the perfect blend of us.

Around eight weeks postpartum, I felt much, much better. It wasn't as painful anymore to move around, Chance was getting healthier and growing so fast I couldn't believe it. Once I'd gotten the green light from Dr. Maxine, I decided to whip my butt in just enough shape to fit into the wedding dresses I was scheduled to try on in July. Fortunately, it didn't take me too long to get back into shape, though I did have loose skin that was never going to go away unless I had plastic surgery. Cane swore he loved it because it was literal proof that I was his, but I legit hated it.

Before I knew it, my college graduation had arrived. I worked tirelessly and consistently. I did it, through all the sleepless nights and ups and downs, and everyone was there.

"Oh, honey. I'm so proud of you!" Mom was jumping up and down with me wrapped in her arms, hugging me tight after the graduation ceremony.

"Thanks, Mom."

She released me, and I looked at Dad, who had a bouquet of flowers in his hands. "For my baby girl," he said, offering the peonies to me. Peonies had become my favorite. Since I had spent more time in the house during the pregnancy, and even more so after having Chance, I decorated the house a lot, giving it different accents and making it fresher. Flowers were one of my favorite ways to spruce things up.

I accepted the flowers and hugged my dad then I looked to where Cane, Lora, and Miss Cane were. Miss Cane had Chance in her arms, smiling at me. Cane had his fingertips tucked in his front pockets and was watching me. He wore a sky-blue button-down with a charcoal tie, and pants to match the tie. His beard had been trimmed down so that it was just a light dusting of hair along his jawline. His sleeves were rolled up, showcasing his beautiful ink.

I swear, my fiancé was the most handsome man in the world. Every time I looked at him, a frenzy of butterflies went haywire inside me. I went up to him, and he stretched his arms open, pulling me close.

"Look at you," he breathed in my hair. "My baby. I'm so proud of you."

I picked my head up, and he dropped a kiss on my cheek. When he opened his arms, I turned to Lora and Miss Cane.

"Congrats, chick," Lora sighed over my shoulder as she hugged me. I squeezed her back and then handed my flowers to Cane, nabbing Chance out of Miss Cane's arms. My adorable baby smiled at me when I cooed to him, like he was just as proud of me as everyone else.

"Your mama made it, little baby," I sang, nuzzling my nose on his cheek. "Yep, I'm going to use this degree to take care of you and show you that anything is possible!"

Chance made an innocent noise and my eyes watered up, filling with warm tears. His little hand grabbed my cheek, but before the dam could break, I hugged him to my chest and rubbed his back.

"What do you say we eat at my place?" Cane asked. "All of us," he offered, focusing on my parents. "I ordered food from a good friend of mine who is catering food from his Italian restaurant."

"Sure. Sounds good," Dad agreed with a head bob.

When we got home, the Italian food was already waiting for us, set up on Cane's large dinner table. We all ate and celebrated. Lora filled me in on her wedding planning. Granted, she always had an update about it, but I didn't mind. She was doing a great job, and I'd much rather spend my time with the baby. The color scheme was going to be gold, beige, and ivory, and I couldn't wait to see it all come together.

I would be going for my first dress fitting in just a few weeks, but I still had a few pounds to shed before then.

It was getting surreal. In exactly four months, I was going to be a bride—and not just any bride: *Quinton Cane's* bride. That alone was special. I looked up at my fiancé and grinned as he held Chance. As if he felt my eyes, he picked his head up and smiled right back at me.

"I love you," he mouthed.

"I love you more," I mouthed back.

CHAPTER 19

KANDY

ONE THING I loved was that no matter the circumstances, my parents visited as often as they could. Unless Dad had to work late, they were always there and always hogging Chance.

Mom constantly came bearing new gifts, like bottles and clothes and even playsets. She loved spoiling him. They loved their grandson so much and had definitely put their differences with Cane behind them for the most part.

"I know I say it all the time, but he's perfect," Mom said while we all sat in the den. She was holding Chance, watching him sleep.

"He seriously is," Lora agreed. "I love his chunky little face."

Miss Cane and Mom hummed in agreement while Dad and Cane sipped their beers.

"Oh, Kandy, I found the perfect decorations for the arch," Lora said, coming to sit next to me. "I don't want to show you just yet. I want you to be surprised, but just know it is going to be amazing!"

"I really love how you are handling everything for the

wedding. Seriously, with Chance and schoolwork, I don't think I would have had time to do much of anything as far as planning it."

"You sure? I feel like I'm being an overbearing bitch." Lora's voice was playful, but in her eyes I could tell she was really worried that she was overstepping.

"No—not at all. I swear. You run your ideas by me, and I agree or disagree. I like that! Also makes me feel less stressed."

"I like that you're doing it too," Mom chimed in. "Knowing Kandy, she would have just gone to the courthouse and gotten it over with. She needs something special."

"Same with Cane, and I wasn't having it!" Lora declared. "I got your back, Mrs. Jennings. This wedding is going to be one for the books."

"Is wedding planning something you'd like to pursue for a career?" Dad asked. "Totally fits you, with all the wild hair colors and your go-getter mentality."

"Hmm...I don't know. I do like decorating things and piecing stuff together, but I'm looking at this as more of a hobby thing. It's fun, but doing it for real means I'd have to deal with bridezillas, and I'm not up for that shit."

Dad laughed. "I guess I can understand that."

"You'd probably give an annoying bride a black eye right before her wedding day," Cane joked.

I snickered at that one. "I definitely see that happening," I teased, nudging her with my elbow.

Lora simply shrugged. "Hey, it is what it is. I'm a bitch with an attitude."

I really was happy having Lora do most of the handy work. All I had to do was say "Yes" or "No" to her options, and she was handling the rest. She and Cane were setting up the guest list, but I did tell her to add two people to it that I hadn't seen in years, as well as Frankie and Clay, if he wanted to tag along with her. Lora, Mom, Miss Cane, and I were going to spend a day trying on a collection of dresses I'd picked out at a local boutique, and I was super excited about it because it was something hands-on I could do, and one step closer to the big day.

∽

LATER THAT NIGHT, when my parents left to go home and Cane and I were in our room with Chance, Cane brought something up that I was not expecting.

"You know what?" he asked.

"What?"

"There's been something that has been bothering me for a while now. It's almost like you've forgotten about it, or let it go, but I still think about it," he said, and his eyes had changed, his face slightly more serious. "It comes to mind at least once a week for me."

"What is it?" I asked, bringing Chance over my shoulder to burp him.

"Well, the shit that happened at Notre Dame, with you losing your scholarship because of the people who ratted us out..."

"Oh, God." I groaned and closed my eyes for a split second. I hated reliving that horror. "I haven't forgotten about that. Trust me," I mumbled.

"But you damn sure don't talk about it." Cane extended his arms, reaching for Chance. I lowered him, carefully shifting him from my arms to his dad's. Cane cuddled him into his chest and rubbed his back to get him to burp, and there was always something about that gesture that made me all fuzzy and warm on the inside. Chance burped and his eyes drooped. Cane rocked him softly, putting his focus back on me.

"I don't like thinking about that for a reason, Cane. When I do, I just get angry all over again. I used to constantly wish I could go back in time to stand my ground a little more, you know? I guess I just felt like I had no options back then; I didn't want you outed or your reputation ruined. If it happened right now, I would absolutely call them out."

Cane sighed. "Well, you know how I am, and you know it's hard for me to let shit go." He looked me in the eyes, and that look alone—the one where his eyes turned a slight shade darker and his eyebrows were drawn together—said it all. He'd done something that he knew I wouldn't be pleased to know.

"Oh, no. Cane, what did you do?" I straightened my back and he looked away, turning with Chance in his arms.

"It's not that bad," he mumbled. "Not harsh enough, really."

"Just spit it out."

He faced me again, exhaling. "Okay, look. When that shit happened, you were so upset, and I'd never heard you get so mad at me before. You'd never called me and broken down like that—or even talked to me that way. It was years ago, honestly, and I didn't want to tell you because I did what I did out of anger…"

"What did you do?" I demanded.

"Kandy, that school let you take all the flack for what happened between us, which was fucking personal and happened off campus. And what really pissed me off was that they didn't contact me about what happened to confirm it, and they didn't even give you a fair chance to stay, and you worked your ass off for that scholarship. It was all some made-up, textbook bullshit about school conduct, and to be honest, they played favorites. You were new, and not many people knew you, but they knew the kids who ratted on you very well, knew they were good at the sports they played, and they chose their side. I looked into those kids, and the girl was a big player on your team, and the boy, Brody," he gritted through clenched teeth, "he was a good football player. They chose their athletes over standard."

"Oh my gosh, Cane. Seriously, what are you getting at?" I pushed up on my knees as he turned for the bassinet, placing Chance inside it carefully. Chance was fully asleep now, his little mouth hanging wide open like he worked a nine-to-five job.

"Look, I called your mom around the time it'd happened and asked her if she could look into the board hearing, the coach, and those students. Mindy didn't hesitate. She was still fired up about it, and she knew you weren't going to act on it, so she took matters into her own hands." He lowered his gaze, drawing in a slow breath. "Let's just say your mother is a damn good lawyer."

"What do you mean?"

"I mean...for her to only make one simple threat with big words, and for the board to actually take it seriously and to follow through, she's damn good. She listened to that hearing, looked into the school's code of conduct, and she talked to a few of your former teammates. Several of them said Sophie was not nice to you at all. She insisted that your former teammate and that boy were bullying you, and their first rule in their code of conduct is to treat everyone as their neighbor, and to not shun those whom are different. Basically, the school is supposed to have a zero tolerance policy on bullying, and your coach didn't think to mention that when she gave her testimony. Your mom said she wanted the coach fired and the girl and the boy to have their scholarships revoked too, and if the school refused, she guaranteed she would make a spectacle out of it . Of course it was an empty threat, because she didn't want to drag you through any more hell, but she sure as shit made it feel real."

"Wow." I was so shocked to hear that. "Wait...when did all of this even happen? You weren't close with my parents anymore after I got kicked out."

"It was back when your parents and I weren't on very good terms. I called, and she picked up the phone. It was the day when you didn't tell them where you were after the school kicked you out. I told her you were fine, and when I told her you didn't deserve what they'd done to you, she agreed. She went on a rant about it, saying she wanted to do something. So we talked about it...and she took action. She clearly told me she wasn't doing this for me, but that it was for you. She kept me updated, though, and I was glad to hear something had happened a few months later. So much was happening to us, and it never felt like the right time to tell you what we did. I've been meaning to talk to you about it but never could remember when it was an appropriate time."

My mind was boggled. I couldn't believe this. "So Brody and Sophie lost their scholarships?"

"Brody's got revoked, and Sophie was pulled from the team and expelled. She can't even say she has a degree from Notre Dame. I don't think anything is worse than that."

"Oh my God, Cane." My words came out winded. I climbed off the bed. "You did that?" I didn't know whether to be really fucking happy and glad my man had my back, or upset because he may have possibly ruined their lives. I wasn't a spiteful person. I believed Karma would do her job, so I left it alone. That was how I found peace in that situation.

"I couldn't leave it alone. And technically, your mom was the one who got it all in motion. She looks out for you a lot more than you realize. She always has."

I lowered my head, blinking my tears away.

"I normally keep a level head when it comes to things like that, but when it comes to *you*, I lose it. I never want to see you hurt, and if there is a way I can safely and legally give payback, trust me, I will." He grabbed my hands and brought them up to his lips to kiss them. "That goes for you and my son."

He pulled me in for a hug, and I closed my eyes, hugging him back. "I'm going to end up marrying a madman."

He belted out a hearty laugh, and with my ear to his chest, I could hear the laughter and steady rhythm of his heartbeat. "A madman who loves you."

"I guess I don't talk about it because it's in the past. I can't change anything now, so it's pointless to even get upset about it anymore. What they did was wrong…but it led me to you again."

"Yeah, but at a cost. And if it hadn't been for me going there, it never would have happened."

"I don't want to think like that. If you hadn't come, we wouldn't be where we are now." I pulled away, looking toward the soft-green bassinet. "We wouldn't have Chance."

Cane looked with me and sighed. "No," he murmured with a smile. "I suppose we wouldn't."

CHAPTER 20

Cane

TIME WENT BY EFFORTLESSLY, every moment of it unforgettable. Of course, there were tough days. Kandy was raising the baby and was new at the whole mom thing. I didn't know shit about being a dad, so I winged as much of it as I could. Still, my son and Kandy were my number one priority. Their happiness was important to me, and I made sure they were content at all costs.

Chance was something else. I loved that kid so much more than I had loved anyone in this world. Don't get me wrong—I loved Kandy, and I loved my family, but those were two different kinds of loves. My love for Chance felt...*unreal*, so to speak. I mean, there were nights when I looked at him and wondered how I was so lucky to have him. After everything I'd done and all I'd been through, I couldn't believe that the result was this beautiful boy, who I knew I didn't deserve.

My son was a ray of light in my world, just like his mother was to me. My son gave me even more purpose than before. I had so many plans for him, like how I'd be at every practice and every game I could attend when he started playing sports. I would support him 100 percent, no matter what I had going on in my life or at work. He was everything to me, and after having him, it was hard picturing a life without the little man.

Before I knew it, September had arrived, the day before Kandy's bachelorette party. I had many male friends and colleagues but refused to have a bachelor party. I wasn't up for it. I would have rather worked than have to awkwardly watch a stripper take her clothes off, desperate for attention that I didn't want to give.

Lora wouldn't let up for Kandy, though. She wanted her to have a spa day at a nice hotel, so she'd booked it way in advance. I specifically told my sister no strippers or dancers. I meant that shit, too. No man was about to come around my future wife, swinging his dick in her face.

I had to admit, though, Lora had done a great job with the setup of the wedding. It was going to be held at our house, in the back yard, with all of our loved ones around. As I walked around, noticing the bouquet of flowers in certain corners and splashes of gold everywhere, it hit me that this was really, *really* happening. In less than forty-eight hours, I was going to be marrying the love of my life. Something about that choked me up, and not in a bad way.

Mama decided to give Kandy a break, so she took Chance for a walk. There were people in the house, setting up for the wedding, but with Lora driving all around the city in preparation for it, as well as Kandy's bachelorette day tomorrow, we were alone for the first time in a while. Walking upstairs, I rounded the corner to get to our bedroom.

When I was inside, I heard the shower running, so I closed the door and then pulled my shirt over my head. Kandy was humming a song under the stream of water, and from here, I could see her sexy silhouette. After getting undressed, I walked to the shower, opening the door and stepping inside.

"Cane," she gasped. "What are you doing?"

"Taking a shower with Mrs. Cane," I rumbled.

She grinned up at me, draping her arms around my neck. Her brown eyes zeroed on mine, and I felt my cock twitch on her thigh.

"You ready for the big day?" I asked.

"Yeah. Are you?"

"I've been ready ever since I asked you." My eyes dropped to her full, pouty lips. I wanted to taste those lips so bad—suck the plump bottom one into my mouth and graze it between my teeth.

As if she read my mind, her head tipped up, and I clasped her chin, kissing her deep. She moaned, shoving her fingers through my hair, as if she'd been waiting all day for this kiss. Groaning, I picked her up in my arms, and she knew exactly what to do. Her legs went around my hips, and I pressed her back to the wall, pushing between her legs.

Any other time, I would have held off, waited a little, but not this time. No, this time I was hungry for her. *Ravenous.* I found the perfect position and thrust my cock into her. Her back bowed against the wall, mouth parting on top of mine. She gasped louder as I stroked faster, her eyes both surprised and entranced. She had no idea why I was being such an animal, or why she liked it so much.

To be frank, I didn't know why either at first, but when I thought about it, I realized that it was me leaving my mark. Creating a stamp for this moment. This would be our last time fucking as fiancé and fiancée. By Saturday afternoon, she was officially going to be my *wife* and we had to walk into this matrimony with a bang.

So yes, I fucked my future wife in the shower. Yes, I sucked on my future wife's neck, and cupped her ass in my hands while my cock swelled up inside her. Yes, I made her mine, because tomorrow, she wasn't going to be Kandy Jennings anymore. She was going to be Kandy *Cane*. *My* Kandy Cane, and the idea of that sparked a fire in me so intense that I couldn't let go.

When I reached my final pump upwards, I pulled out and came between our stomachs.

She sighed loudly, holding onto me as I jerked with each spurt of release. I huffed a laugh, and she broke out in a smile. When I placed her down, we rinsed off and then washed, but before we got out, I turned her toward me and asked, "You're mine, right?"

"I'm yours," she replied.

"Always?"

She smiled. "Forever, babe."

I never got tired of those words coming out of her mouth.

~

"I can't wait to see the final look on Saturday," I said after we got dressed. "I have no doubt you'll be stunning...not that you aren't already."

"And I'm sure you'll be dangerously handsome." She chewed on her bottom lip, and then looked away, getting quiet. I knew that look all too well.

"What's wrong?"

"I'm nervous about leaving Chance for five whole days for the honeymoon."

"Why?"

"I don't know. I've never been away from him for that long, Cane. It's going to be weird. Now that I have him, it's weird picturing life without him. How did I survive before?" She laughed.

"No idea how either of us did," I chuckled. "But you pumped enough, right?"

"Yes, but—"

"No buts, Kandy. It's a short honeymoon to Paris. If the fridge is loaded with your milk, he'll be okay. Trust me, Chance will be fine. Your mom and my mom are here. They won't let anything happen to him."

"I know," she sighed. "I know." She walked up to me, hugging me. I hugged her back, looking around our closet, at her clothes on one side and mine on the opposite. "Are you ready to spend forever with me?" she asked, her cheek pressed to my chest.

"Forever and always, baby."

"Are you just saying that?"

"No, I'm not just saying it." I reached down and cradled her face in my hands, putting her eyes on mine. "I mean it." I gave her a full, deep kiss on the lips. "Saturday will be amazing, and you will look amazing, and you'll be surrounded by amazing people. *Amazing*, you got it?"

She nodded. "I already have the jitters."

"As do I, but we've been through so much shit. It's only right that we meet one another at the altar, right?"

She blushed, revealing a beautiful white smile. "Right."

CHAPTER 21

KANDY

WEDDING DAY

THE DAY I'd been waiting for—*dreamed* of—had arrived. I thought it would never come.

Before this day, I got to really unwind and relax at the bachelorette party. Honestly, it wasn't a bachelorette party at all. It was a chill, relaxing day with lots of snacks, food, drinks, facials, and massages. I shared a spa day with Frankie, Lora, and Mom, and to my utter surprise, Morgan and Gina showed up at the spa, too.

"Oh my gosh!" I wailed as soon as I saw them. I rushed away from the massage table and wrapped them both up in my arms.

"Look at you, you fine-ass woman!" Morgan hollered. She looked me all over and then hugged me again. "Didn't I tell you to stay in touch?"

"I know, I know!" I laughed. "Things got intense in my life

after that whole thing with Brody and Sophie." I waved that topic off, focusing on Gina, who was smiling so hard. "Gina! You look so damn pretty!"

"You're one to talk! You're glowin' like the sun, babe!"

Ugh. It was so good to have all my favorite girls around me. I was glad Lora sent them the invitation, and that they came early to see me. I needed that one-on-one time with them. I felt bad that I hadn't kept in touch with Morgan and Gina much. I mean, yes, we did have a group chat, but we hardly used it. And back when the stabbing happened, they did text me a lot, but I would never respond, and eventually they stopped trying. I just wasn't in the headspace for conversation.

During my spa day, I explained it all to them and promised to keep in touch for good this time. They were happy that I invited them to the wedding, and I was glad they came. I loved those girls so much. Frankie got to know them too, and could see why I'd become so tight with them while at Notre Dame.

I was nervous about the big day. I hoped everything would be perfect and run smoothly. My hair was done, my dress was on. I was in the extra room Cane let me call mine, sitting in front of the vanity, my heart pounding.

The sun was out that fall Saturday, the leaves on the trees in many shades of yellow, orange, and rustic brown.

I stood from the chair and looked into the mirror, running my hands over the creamy dress. It was exactly what I wanted, and fit me just right. I decided to go with an embroidered, spaghetti-strapped dress, made of a mixture of chiffon and satin. It was simple, and if anyone knew anything about me, they knew the simple things were usually my favorite things.

A knock sounded on the door, and I looked back. Lora popped her head in with a big smile. Her cotton-candy pink hair was braided into a crown and her makeup was absolutely flawless. I'd never seen her wear much makeup, but it was a natural glam, and she looked spectacular.

"You ready, munchkin?" she asked, sliding through the crack of the door and closing it. Even her dress was pretty—a simple, mid-sleeve gold dress, the bottom half made of tulle.

"I think so," I breathed, running my slick palms down the front of my dress. "Do I look okay?"

She blinked rapidly, her thick lashes batting. "Kandy…you look like a fucking goddess. I mean—" she scoffed, "you are stunning, babe. Q is going to flip, and by flip, I mean he's going to be drooling all down those lush tits of yours tonight." She walked my way, and I laughed, turning to look in the mirror again.

"Are there already a lot of people here?" I asked as she fixed the loose tendrils of my hair. It was in an updo, and styled with a tiara made of pearls and real diamonds, while two strands dangled in front of my face. Lora had hired a hair stylist and a makeup artist for me, and they came this morning and made me up like a princess.

"Oh, yeah. I think everyone you guys invited is here. Rich people are prompt motherfuckers."

"My parents too?"

Just as I asked, there was another knock on the door. Lora went to open it, peeking out first before letting the person in. Mom sashayed into the room with a big smile, Chance in her arms. Frankie followed in behind her, gawking as soon as she saw me. When Chance spotted me, he grinned and reached for me with a tiny grunt, but Mom held onto him a little tighter.

"Oh, no, little man," Lora said, scooping Chance up in her arms. "Can't ruin your mama's dress! She's gotta be pretty all day, and we don't need baby vomit all over her!"

While Lora taunted and teased Chance, Mama focused on me. As she looked me over, her eyes shimmered. "Oh, honey." She pressed a hand to her mouth, fighting tears. "You look so beautiful. Like an angel."

I bit back my tears as she came toward me, giving me a tight squeeze. "Thank you," I murmured over her shoulder. Lora smiled at us in her corner briefly before looking at Chance and pushing his hair back.

"Seriously, though, K.J. I'm digging this dress, hard. I mean, when you sent me the picture when you tried it on, I knew it was the one, but now that I see it in person...yeah, this really is the one!"

I couldn't fight my smile. "It's pretty comfortable too, surprisingly." I looked at Chance as he looked at me. He wanted me to hold him so badly. "Aww, look at him in his little tux!" I cooed. I reached for him but Lora held up a hand.

"Kandy, no. This little boy just had a bottle, which means he can blow at any time. He can't hold a thing down, and you know it!"

"I just want to hug him!" I laughed, and she gave me a momentary look of defeat before letting me grab him.

"Fine."

I kissed Chance on the nose, then pressed my forehead to his as he made tiny noises. When I gave him a little squeeze, he let out a tiny grunt and frowned. Mom and Frankie laughed.

"Stubborn like his mother, I see," Mom teased with a laugh.

"He's just like her," Frankie added.

Lora quickly took Chance from me and handed him back to Mom. "Okay, you can hug him more later. The wedding is about to start, ladies. Mrs. Jennings, I'm assuming you and my mom are on baby duty?"

"Yes, we are. We've got you, right, chunky-lumpkins?" Mom was baby-talking to him, and of course Chance got a kick out of it, grinning and kicking. He always did.

"And Mr. Jennings is still at the bottom of the staircase waiting for the bride?" Lora asked.

"He was there when I came up. I'm sure he hasn't gone anywhere."

"And Frankie, you've got that camera ready for some personal pictures?"

Frankie held up her phone. "Hell yeah. Best camera phone out there!"

"Okay, good! Let's get this wedding started then, shall we?" Lora turned to open the door, and Mom and Frankie walked out, Mom hiking Chance on her hip.

"Let me know if you need anything," Mom called over her shoulder.

"I will, Mom!"

She smiled on her way out, and Lora watched them go before coming back to me. "Okay." She held my upper arms, looking me all over. "You literally look like a million bucks, which is good because that's about how much this entire wedding cost. Well, maybe more like *two* million, but who's counting, right?"

"Oh my God, Lora! Two million dollars? Are you serious?"

"What? Everything had to look good, okay? I wasn't letting my brother, who I thought would never marry *anyone*, have a half-assed wedding! And you, my dear, deserve the world. Don't think about the money. Just live in the moment, okay? Besides, it wasn't a million. More like half."

I pressed my lips, giving her a playful eye roll. "Fine. I'll try."

"Good enough. Now, come on. Let's get your ass downstairs."

Lora helped me walked down the marble staircase of our house and on the way down, I noticed the flowers wrapped around the railing and even the petals of peonies, which are my favorite flower. Lora struggled to find them since they weren't exactly in season.

"Nice touch on the flowers," I murmured to her as we walked down.

"Yeah, thanks. They were a bitch to find, so you better enjoy them." She smirked, looking at me through the corner of her eye.

On our way down, I saw my dad standing at the bottom of the staircase with a tuxedo on. I have to admit, I wasn't positive he'd be there. I had mentioned that I wanted him to walk me down the aisle and hand me over to Cane several weeks ago, and I could tell the idea of handing me over didn't sit well with him, with his throat clearing and head shaking, but reluctantly he said he would do it. For me and Chance.

"Well, Mr. Jennings, don't you look swell!" Lora chimed when we got closer.

Dad put on a small smile, and when his eyes shifted over to me, they stretched wider. He looked me up and down, shock taking over him. "Wow," he huffed.

"What?" I asked nervously.

"I knew my daughter was gorgeous before, but today...you are breathtaking, kid."

I felt heat swim up to my cheeks. "Thanks, Dad."

"All righty. Here is your bride." Lora released my arm to hand me over to Dad, and Dad hooked his arm through mine.

"Got her."

"I'm going to go out back and make sure everything is in order and that the band is ready. You guys will wait here until I come back."

"The band?" I asked, deadpan.

"Yes, the *band*, Kandy. Look, a lot of shit is going to surprise you today, so just get ready." She pointed at me. "It'll be the best day you've ever had!"

Dad and I laughed while Lora turned on her wedges and walked through the foyer. When she was around the corner, Dad said, "She's a hot mess."

"She really is. But she's a good person. Has a good heart."

"Must be a Cane thing." Dad shrugged. "They all have good hearts, deep down. It's just a matter of getting past all the layers to see it, I suppose." He sighed. "She did a great job. I took a look around earlier. The wedding will be beautiful."

I smiled. "I'm glad." I shifted on my heels. "Dad...thank you for doing this."

I peered up, and he pressed his lips. He'd shaved his beard away totally. His face was the cleanest I'd seen it in months.

Normally he rocked his scruff. "I love you," he asserted. "You and Chance are my family, and all I want is for you to be happy." I watched his throat bob as he said, "And when you're with Cane, I see it. The light in your eyes. Your fire, and how alive you are when he's nearby. He wakes you up—awakens a part of your soul that only *he* can touch. Who am I to stand in the way of that anymore?"

Tears crept to the corners of my eyes, but I blinked rapidly, trying to fan them away. "Oh, God."

Dad chuckled. "Don't cry on me. I can't risk Lora's wrath for messing up the bride's makeup."

I giggled, then rested my head on his arm. "I love you so much, Dad. I always will. Like Cane said, you're the number one man in my life, for life."

He smiled smugly, but I noticed the way his eyes glistened. "Oh, trust me, I know," he said, then he gave me a wink.

Music began to play. Live music. A band was playing a wedding march melody.

Lora appeared, trotting around the corner. "Okay, you guys ready?" she asked breathlessly.

"Nervous," I admitted.

"Oh, don't be," she said, meeting up to my side. "This is *your* big day, and remember that at the end of that aisle is a man who loves you and can't wait to make you his wife."

"Okay." I drew in a breath before exhaling. "Let's do this."

"Thatta girl." She winked before stepping in front of us. "Follow me."

We followed after Lora, my arm linked through Dad's. My heart thundered with each step we took, moving closer and closer to the music. Before I knew it, we were at the end of the hallway, where the double doors were perched wide open. From where we stood, I could see the lined up chairs and the tall white arch in the large backyard, past the pool.

We followed Lora down the cement steps that led to a gold

runway, covered in creamy white flower petals. I felt Dad tense up as everyone looked back at us, all of them standing and staring.

"Oh boy," he muttered.

There were so many eyes—and most of them were stranger's eyes. I'd never met half of these people, but I visually sifted through the crowd until I found my first familiar face. Miss Cane was standing at the end of the second row, holding Chance. She smiled at me, and relief swam through me as I smiled back. I looked at the row in front of hers and saw Mom next, who had her hands clasped, holding them above her lips. Her eyes were filled with tears—I could see that from where I stood. I smiled at Mom and noticed Frankie a few seats over, waving like a damn maniac. Morgan and Gina were next to her, grinning as I made my way up.

I giggled quietly and looked away before I got too distracted and allowed my best friend to make a fool out of me in front of everyone.

Finally, my eyes shifted over to the middle, right at the end of the altar, and there he was.

Mr. Cane.

My Cane.

He had his hands clasped in front of him, and my God, he looked so, so handsome. His ivory tuxedo, gold bowtie, and gold vest looked amazing on him and fit him well. His hair had been trimmed, and I could tell it'd been fingered with gel, a sleek look that only he could pull off. His beard was gone now, his face bare and clean. His gray-green eyes locked on mine, pulled me in, and from that moment forward, he was all I could focus on.

I didn't care about the crowd.

Didn't care that everyone was gawking over me.

Didn't care that my heart was about to beat out of my chest due to my nerves.

He was right there, waiting for me like he'd promised he would be. His eyes were full of wonder and surprise and awe, and

I sucked in a breath, holding in most of the air until I was at the step that led up to my Cane.

The arch was beautiful, swathed in white, gold, and beige flowers. Creamy drapes hung down from the beam, lightly shifting with the fall breeze.

I lowered my gaze to Cane's again, and as the minister requested my dad to hand me over to Cane, Dad didn't hesitate like I thought he would. I peered up at my dad, who cupped my face and kissed my forehead. He smiled down at me before putting his focus on Cane.

"Take care of my girl," Dad murmured.

"Always," Cane said.

Dad gave a slight nod, offering my hand to Cane's, and when our hands connected, I released the trapped breath in my lungs. *Finally.*

"I don't even have the words to describe how I feel right now," Cane murmured as the minister began talking. His eyes were lined with tears, and when he blinked, the tears spilled down both his cheeks. "You are, without a doubt, the most beautiful woman I have ever laid eyes on."

My heart boomed, and I couldn't fight the tears that left me too. Cane wasn't a man who cried, I knew that, but he was emotional in this moment, just as much as I was. We knew getting married was a big step. But we were here—right here—doing this. Together. After fighting so hard, we were here. We'd made it. And if I thought what he said before was sweet…well, his vows blew me away.

"Kandy…I've told you before and I'll tell you again. I love you. I love you so much it hurts sometimes. There was a point in my life when I almost lost you, and when it happened I, um…I didn't know what to do with myself." He looked up, and his eyes were watery again. I gave him an encouraging smile, letting him know it was okay. "I thought I had loved you hard before, but when you're about to lose someone, that love changes. I realized that if

I'd lost you, my world wouldn't have been the same. I wouldn't have my soulmate standing right here with me. I wouldn't have my beautiful son, who we fought so hard to have. I wouldn't be able to wake up to your smile, or your angelic face. I wouldn't even know what true happiness was if you hadn't come into my life. I was drowning, but you pulled me up for air—gave me *life*, baby—and I never want to lose that. I promise to be here for eternity, Kandy. I promise to put a smile on your face every single day, even on your lowest days. I promise to be here during every stage of your life as you grow. To hold your hand when you don't have enough courage. To push you through, and help you gain whatever motivation you need when you want to accomplish something. My heart will beat only for you, because my heart belongs *to you*. I vow to be here with you for the rest of my life, till my dying breath. You are mine, and I am yours, and it will be that way forever."

Somewhere during his vows, I'd lost it, and had I not been the center of attention, I would have been a blubbering mess. Of course I cried—what woman wouldn't? But I also smiled and felt immense comfort and satisfaction with his words. Who knew Quinton Cane could be so romantic?

The ceremony was beautiful, really. My vows couldn't top his by a long shot. Everything he said, I'd pretty much thought, only he said it better.

Before I knew it, the minister was saying, "You may now kiss your bride, Mr. Cane," and Cane wrapped me up in his arms and kissed me. You better believe I gave this kiss my all. Out of all the kisses we shared, all the moments when we touched and loved, this one felt most important. Didn't matter that my parents were in the crowd watching. I loved this man with all my heart, and every single person watching was going to know it.

"I now pronounce you husband and wife! Friends, please join me in congratulating Mr. and Mrs Cane!" the minister cheered, and we kissed even harder then, taking a break to laugh before going in for one more taste.

Cane and I had gone through so much— experienced so many ups and down and broken moments. At one point, I thought we would never be, yet there we were. Right where we belonged. I was in his arms, and he was holding me like his life depended on it, kissing me so passionately, so achingly deep, I could feel it in my core.

While we kissed, everyone clapped for us. I heard Frankie whooping and hollering, and there were even a few whistles going around. When our kiss broke, I looked at my parents and was glad to see they were both smiling. Everyone here was happy for us, even the people I didn't know, and that meant a lot to me.

EPILOGUE

Kandy

I THINK the reception was my favorite part. There was live music and so much food and cake. Yes, cake. After spending the last three months not eating any sugar so I could fit in my dress, I devoured it, and it felt so damn good.

I shared dances with Cane. I shared dances with my dad. I even shared dances with my little prince, Chance. I met several of Cane's most trusted colleagues, and most of them were pretty cool guys. The music was loud and pulsed through me, and I didn't care that I'd sweat my hair out, or that my elegant bun was toppling down. I was having fun and celebrating my marriage to a man I loved wholly and dearly. A man who I'd suffered losses with, as well as many wins.

It wasn't too long before I decided to go back for my second slice of cake, but as the server handed it to me, Lora appeared over my shoulder. "Hey, Kandy. There's a guy at the front door who says he needs to speak with you."

I narrowed my eyes. "What? Who?"

"I don't know, but he's cute. He said his name's Brody. Should I let him in?"

"What the hell?" I placed my plate down and then looked across the room at Cane. He was standing by the champagne table, talking to a few of his colleagues. "Uh, no…I'll go out. Keep Cane occupied, 'kay?"

"Sure, yeah."

I grabbed a handful of my dress and hurried to the steps that led up to the pool. My heels clicked on the marble as I walked through the house, and as soon as I opened the door, sure enough, Brody Hawks was there. When he spotted me, a smile stretched across his lips, but I could tell it was hard for him to do.

He looked…*different*. For starters, he had a beard now. Scruffy and dark. His eyes looked empty too, like he hardly ever slept. I couldn't fight the frown that swept over my face as I looked him over, stepping out and shutting the door behind me.

"Wow," he breathed. "You look amazing."

"Brody?" I took a step closer. "What are you doing here?"

"I um…well, it's going to sound crazy trying to explain it," he said with an awkward chuckle.

My brows rose out of curiosity, but I folded my arms, waiting for him to finish.

"Look, Kandy…I'll be completely honest with you. I don't want to waste your time, but this felt like the only time I'd be able to say it." He sighed. "I came to apologize about what happened at Notre Dame. Back then, you wouldn't have known it, but I was on some really heavy stuff. I tried to keep up my good boy appearances, but when I partied with the team, I did a lot of drinking and experimented with a lot of drugs that messed with my head and my morals. I know this won't change the way you feel about me, but after what happened, I couldn't stop thinking about it. Clearly, you couldn't either, because I got served and kicked out." His laugh was dry.

"Brody, how did you even find out where I was?" I asked.

"Oh…I, uh, looked into that Cane guy. I saw he had moved his office to Charlotte a few months ago, and I figured he still kept in touch with you after everything. I thought if I could get through to him, I could reach you."

"Reach me? To apologize?"

"Yes." He did a long blink. "But…I didn't reach him at first. I got his assistant instead. She was persistent with telling me no, but I kept calling. Kept asking if I could talk to Mr. Cane. I want to say it took me a solid two weeks before she finally caved and listened to me, and I told her everything. I told her what I did to you, and how fucked up it was. I told her that you didn't deserve what happened to you at all, and that you were one of the smartest, nicest girls I'd ever met and that I ruined your life. She heard me out, told me she'd patch me through to Mr. Cane…and he promptly told me to fuck off," he laughed.

I snorted. I could totally picture Cane telling him to fuck off in the subtlest of ways.

"But I got to him before he hung up. I told him I wanted to apologize to you and him in person. He told me there was no need to apologize to him. He'd settled the score long ago. But he said there was still a chance for me to ask for your forgiveness."

"When was this call with him?"

"Two weeks ago."

"So, you're here because you're miserable, is that it?" I demanded. "You think that by coming here it will solve all your problems?"

"No, Kandy, I swear…that's not it. I mean—what I did to you was foul, man. I—I think about it all the time. Even when I was in the clear, after you got kicked out, I kept thinking about it, but I kept drinking and snorting and smoking, hoping I would get rid of that guilt. When I got kicked out, all of that stopped, and I was left with no choice but to be swallowed by the guilt. Listen, I've never done anything like that to anyone. I was in a very low place in my life and listening to the wrong people. I let my anger take hold of me and almost ruined the future of a girl who only wanted to do good things. Because of it, I ruined my future and any plans I had of creating a good, stable life."

I looked him over before looking away.

"I just...I want to tell you that I'm sorry, that's all. I mean, I flew all the way from Texas to Charlotte, just to tell you how sorry I am. I made this a mission, because I couldn't live with the guilt anymore. I couldn't sleep knowing I'd ruined someone like you."

His eyes glistened from the lights on the patio. He looked nothing but apologetic, and although a part of me wanted to deny all of it, a better, nicer part of me knew it would have been wrong to do so. As a mother and now a *wife*, I had to set examples. I had to learn to forgive, and realize that everything happens for a reason. If Brody and Sophie hadn't done what they did, I probably wouldn't even have Cane, or Chance, for that matter. I never would have built a bigger bond with Lora or Miss Cane, and I definitely wouldn't have found my peace in different ways.

I took a step forward. "Brody, I appreciate you coming all this way to tell me that after so many years. It must have really bothered you, and I'm glad you realized just how messed up it was."

He nodded, lips pressing.

"I have a son now. Did you know that?"

"No way." He smiled, his eyes lighting up a bit.

"Yep. He's six months old. He's a great little human, and one of my goals as a mom is to teach him right from wrong. I want him to learn how to forgive people when they wrong him, even if it hurts. I want him to know that we are all human, and humans are flawed creatures, but if we love and care for one another, maybe it won't all be so bad." I sighed, looking past him at the many cars parked in the roundabout driveway. "For that reason and that reason alone, I forgive you. You came all this way, explained your situation to me, so yes, Brody. I forgive you."

He sighed a big breath of relief, dropping his head. "Thank you."

I smiled softly. "Does Cane know you're here?"

"Sure do." A voice sounded behind me, and I looked back as Cane walked out. He looked Brody over, and Brody straightened his back, watching Cane come out of the door with his chin high.

"Oh my gosh, were you listening to us? What good is Lora?" I asked, playfully punching him.

"What?" Cane smirked, hooking an arm round my waist. "Had to make sure he wasn't making any moves on my *wife*."

"Not at all, sir," Brody assured him. "I appreciate you trusting me with your address. I know it was the last thing you wanted to do."

"Damn right. Not only because I don't like you, but because Kandy's father is here, and he's a mean motherfucker. If he found out that you, the kid who had her expelled from a college she worked her ass off to get into, was here, he would kick your ass twice. Not even kidding. I've been the recipient of a D. Jennings ass-kicking myself."

Brody looked nervous then.

"But, he doesn't know. And I prefer it stays that way," Cane assured him.

Brody relaxed, lowering his gaze.

"What are you doing with your life now?" Cane asked.

"Oh, uh, I work retail as an assistant manager, and I'm an assistant coach for a football team for 8-year-olds."

"Hmm. Retail, huh?"

"You should give him a job," I whispered. "I mean, he came all this way and hounded you. He's clearly dedicated."

Cane didn't bother to lower his voice. "I don't know about that, babe. He might stab me in the back down the road."

I looked over at Brody. "No, he won't. Because if he does that, I'll have to tell my dad all about him. My dad, who happens to be a police sergeant. We wouldn't want that, would we, Brody?"

Brody shook his head. "Nah, we wouldn't."

"All right then," Cane said. "I'll give you a chance. There's a position open at my office in the mailroom. It sounds bad, but it pays much more than retail does, trust me. If you're willing to relocate for a chance to do something better for yourself, email my assistant, let her know."

A smile swept over Brody's face. "Wow, sir. I appreciate the offer, but you don't have to do that. My life isn't bad—I mean, it's not as fancy as yours, but it isn't bad."

"Seventeen dollars an hour," Cane said, and Brody's eyes bulged out of his head. "Plus benefits. Our mailrooms get pretty busy."

"Uh...damn. I'll definitely consider it, then." He laughed and took a step back. "I'll email soon, give you a solid answer."

"Sounds fine."

"Bye, Brody," I called, watching him walk off.

"Thanks for your time." Brody waved goodbye, and when he was out of earshot, Cane said, "I should make him go through the whole process and have them deny his application."

"Oh my gosh, Cane!" I busted out laughing. "No. You're just being an asshole. You meant well, I could tell." I grabbed his arm. "Thank you for doing that—being the bigger person."

"Only for you. I knew you would have wanted that closure. Stuff like that always haunts you one way or another. Besides...I think he's a good kid deep down. Was probably going through some tough shit back then. College is hard. Lots of life changes. Not only that, but he reminds me of myself...minus the drugs. But I was big on drinking in college, and as you can tell from our little experience with Eden St. Claire several months ago, I was not very good to the ladies."

"Yeah, you have a point."

He smiled down at me. "Come on, let's get back to the party."

Cane walked with me into the house, and along the way, we spotted Lora rushing into the kitchen. Cane looked down at me, a dip in his forehead as confusion swept over him, then tugged me to the kitchen, a finger to his lips. Lora was pacing in front of the fridge. When she saw us out of the corner of her eye, she gasped, and her eyes got wide.

"Holy shit, you guys! You can't sneak up on me like that!" she yelled.

"Creep up on you? We're at a party full of people, Lora. What's going on with you?" Cane released my hand, meeting up with his sister.

"Nothing—it's nothing." She shoved her fingers through her hair that was now crinkled from her braids and hanging down past her shoulders.

"You look one edge, Lo," he stated. "You okay?"

"I'm fine. Just—okay, come with me." She grabbed Cane's hand and dragged him to the window that revealed our entire backyard. I met up with them, and Lora pointed out the window. "Do you see that guy over there with the shoulder-length hair? In the black suit and black tie? Do you know him?"

Cane narrowed his eyes a bit. I looked with him and saw a guy standing by the bushes. His hair was brown and wavy, his jaw cut and defined. He was barefaced, his eye swimming over the crowd like he was looking for someone.

"Not that I'm aware of," Cane said, still staring at the man. "Why? Do you know him?"

Lora's eyes widened as she stared out the window. "No," she said quickly. "I just…I didn't see him seated at the wedding. Don't remember checking him off on the list. But now he's here at the reception. You know how popular you are. There are total creeps out there who will crash a wedding to take pictures they can sell."

"Well, shit, Lora, there are a lot of people here at the reception. He could be someone's driver or maybe tagged along with one of the ladies as their guest."

Lora's throat bobbed as she swallowed.

"Lora, are you okay?" I asked. Her face had paled. I'd never seen her like this—not since that time she saw Buck—when she was paralyzed with fear.

"I'm fine." She pressed a hand to her stomach. "I think I've just had too much champagne. Not only that, but I've been up since four this morning getting this wedding ready." She closed her eyes for a brief second, breathing evenly. "Guys, don't let me ruin your night. Go," she insisted, pushing us toward the door. "I'm going to run to the bathroom and hope I don't vomit all over the place."

"All right...text me if you need me." Concern was laced in Cane's voice. I was worried too, but when Lora smiled, I let it go. For now.

Before we reached the crowded area, I said, "I think all this planning has made her stressed and tired. I'm sure she'll feel better once she actually gets to rest."

"Yeah, I think so too. Lora isn't really equipped to run for days. She's like a cat. She needs naps."

I giggled at that.

"She's a paranoid girl, too. She's been that way since she was younger. She always thinks someone is coming after her, probably because of what she went through with Buck as a kid." Cane shrugged. "Once she gets some rest, her anxiety will settle, and she'll be okay."

I nodded, but looked over my shoulder. Lora was standing in front of the door, watching everyone. Cane tugged on my hand, tearing my gaze away, and when we made it back to the reception area, everyone cheered for us.

"How about we let the happy couple share one more solo dance!" the singer said into the microphone, and Cane displayed a full smile.

"Shall we?" He winked at me.

I took his hand, letting him reel me toward him. "Let's."

The singer started singing "*1+1*" by Beyoncé. It was a slow song, but the lyrics defined us in every way. Cane nuzzled his nose in the crook of my neck, and I tossed my head back, laughing. Then I pressed my cheek to his chest, rocking with him, forgetting there were hundreds of eyes on us.

For a split second, I only heard his heartbeat. Felt his skin on mine. His lips in my hair as he kissed me. We were alone on the dance floor, beneath gold lights and stars, and nothing else mattered.

When I opened my eyes, I saw Mom, Miss Cane, Lora, and Dad, who was holding Chance in his arms. They were smiling. Chance was still awake, but barely, his lids drooping.

My eyes shifted over to my girls Morgan, Gina, and Frankie. They were all sipping champagne and laughing their asses off. I spotted Clay not too far off from where Frankie was standing. One of our guests, a younger guy with nice hair and an even nicer smile, came up to Frankie and said something, and Clay's grip tightened around his bottle of beer as Frankie beamed up at the guy. The way he looked at her said it all. I know she said she wanted me to pretend I didn't know a thing, but I'd seen that look before.

Primal. Fierce. Possessive.

Cane had given me that look many, many times before, but there was also adoration. Confusion. He didn't understand his want for her. And that's the funny thing, when it comes to complicated loves like these: they are always hard to understand at first, but if you work through them, weather every storm and conquer your battles, you end up understanding the want. The *need*. You understand that it is worth fighting for.

It starts off as lust, but morphs into so much more.

I picked my head up to look at Cane as the song came to an end. His eyes shimmered from the lights above, his smile content.

Wow...this man. This man was going to be my forever and always. He was going to be my husband, my king, my everything.

Once upon a time, I was a young, hopeless girl with a crush and a desire. A girl who thought there was no chance in hell a man like him would fall for a young, naive girl like me.

Now, I was a woman, with a love worth fighting for and a family I would never take for granted. Now I had him, and we were going to be together for the rest of our lives.

Being Mrs. Cane is something I thought would never happen, yet there I was, right in Quinton Cane's arms, standing as his wife. His *soulmate*

This moment was created by passion, heartbreak, love, and struggles. All of it led up to this perfect day, creating a blissful, unconditional happily ever after for us.

I was his, and he was mine.

So, yes, this was my always.

This was my *forever*.

ACKNOWLEDGMENTS

WOW. WOW, WOW, WOW!

I'm honestly not even sure where to start. There are so many people I want to thank right now.

To my amazing fiancé and soon-to-be husband, Juan, thank you for dealing with me during the many days and nights when I'd hide in the room to get a few chapters in. You took care of the boys when I needed you to and handled it like a boss. You made sure I didn't give up and that's the greatest gift of all. You're an amazing father and I can't wait to marry you!

To Dani Fuselier - girl, I love you so hard. Thank you for letting me blow up your phone with ideas and for getting me pumped about each book, especially during the times when I doubted myself way too much. You're the most supportive, sweetest, amazing person ever and I am so lucky to have you as a friend. I can't wait to meet you soon, because it's going to happen!

To my AMAZING beta readers, Danielle Huffman, MJ Fryer, Love 2 Read, Emma Louise, and Natasha Black, THANK YOU for always giving me your honest feedback and for pushing me in the right direction. I legit would not be able to do this without you! Love you ladies!

To my Pimp It & Sweetheart ARC Team - y'all are too good to me. Too good. I love you all so very much and can't thank you enough for getting the word about Mr. Cane out there for all to know about. I want to hug you all, but for now, take this as one big ol' virtual hug from me to you! I adore and appreciate every single one of you!

To Hang Le for designing the kick-ass covers for the entire Cane series! You are a true gem with a great eye! Your designs slay my soul and I love it!

To Kiezha and Tamsyn for reading over this series and catching all of the grubby little mistakes. Without you, this series would have been trash. Haha. Not kidding. Thank you for all you do for me and for taking time to schedule and pencil me in.

To my Naughty Sweethearts and IG babes! I love y'all sooooo much. You encourage me and push me to keep writing. You all humble me to the core and I would not be here without your amazing support.

And lastly, to every single reader and blogger who gave this series a chance, I can't thank you enough. I really can't. You are the reason I am still able to do this for a living, so thank you for giving me the chance to live my dreams.

AFTERWORD

If you've made it to this part of the book, I want to personally thank you for reading the Cane series. This series had its struggles, but I am so glad I saw it through to the end and that you were on this journey with me. Thank you for loving Kandy Cane as much as I do.

Sign Up For My Newsletter to stay updated and to receive exclusive information about the novella, future books, and so much more!
www.shanorawilliams.com/mailing-list

For updates, teasers, and more fun exclusives:

Follow Me on Instagram @reallyshanora
Join My Facebook Reader Group
Shanora's Naughty Sweethearts

Visit www.shanorawilliams.com for more info and details.
psssttt... by the way, I'm most active on Instagram, my reader group, and Twitter. ;-)

MORE BOOKS BY SHANORA

CANE SERIES
WANTING MR. CANE
BREAKING MR. CANE
LOVING MR. CANE
BEING MRS. CANE

NORA HEAT COLLECTION
CARESS
CRAVE
DIRTY LITTLE SECRET

STANDALONES
TEMPORARY BOYFRIEND
100 PROOF
DOOMSDAY LOVE
DEAR MR BLACK
FOREVER MR. BLACK
INFINITY

SERIES

FIRENINE SERIES
THE BEWARE DUET
VENOM TRILOGY

Most of these titles are available in Kindle Unlimited. Visit www.shanorawilliams.com for more information.

Printed in Great Britain
by Amazon